THE HEALER OF BRIARWOOD

A Montana Gallagher Novel
Tales from Briarwood

MK MCCLINTOCK

A man with a healer's touch.
A woman with a healer's heart.

LARGE PRINT EDITION

Trappers Peak Publishing
Montana

Trappers Peak Publishing
Bigfork, Montana 59911
www.mkmcclintock.com

Publisher's Note: This is a work of fiction. Names, characters, places, and incidents are a product of the author's imagination. Locales and public names are sometimes used for atmospheric purposes. Any resemblance to actual people, living or dead, or to businesses, companies, events, institutions, or locales is completely coincidental.

The Healer of Briarwood; novel/MK McClintock
ISBN: 978-1734864045
LARGE PRINT EDITION

Cover Design by MK McClintock
Cover images:
Woman in black outfit ©Kathy | Adobe Stock
Calm pond in Montana ©Gregory Johnston | Adobe Stock
Woman with hairstyle ©Dragonfly666 | Deposit Photos

draw you in, but the story and the people keep you there." —*Donna McBroom-Theriot*

"Ms. McClintock's stories are adventurous and full of budding romance that transports you back in to a simpler time where the outside world ceases to exist once you open one of her books."
—*My Life, One Story at a Time*

For the healers.
Thank you for your skills, dedication, and sacrifices.

Dearest Reader,

The Gallaghers and the wonderful townsfolk of Briarwood are my family, and it brings us tremendous joy every time we can welcome friends, old and new, into our clan. We have come a long way since *Gallagher's Pride*, and we have shared many wonderful adventures, from shootouts and kidnappings to second chances in love and life.

The Healer of Briarwood highlights the best and worst of humankind, and through it all, it is the hope of a better tomorrow and the love of family and friends that remind us how precious and joyful life can be, even during the darkest of times

I have written this book to stand on its own. You will meet previous characters and read mention of events from the first six Montana Gallagher books. They are here to enhance Brody and Katharine's story, for neither would have his or her own tale without those who came before.

I hope you enjoy reading this romantic western adventure as much as I did writing it, and whether you are here for the first time or returning to Briarwood and Hawk's Peak, the Gallaghers and I thank you for joining us on the journey.

Be well, be kind, and stay bookish!
~MK McClintock

1

Montana Territory
early autumn 1884

BRODY READ OVER the latest issue of *The Lancet* by lamplight in the pre-dawn hours. His focus shifted from a case on typhus to a lecture on the diseases of children as he jotted down a few notes to study later. The quiet hours of morning allowed him to study, for as his mentor once told him, "When a doctor stops learning, he ceases to be a doctor."

Pounding, hard and urgent, shook the front door of his clinic. "Anyone in there?"

Brody pushed away from his desk and rushed to the door. On the other side, a man of small stature struggled to hold a woman in his arms. She lay limp, though Brody could not determine the extent of her injuries in the darkness lurking outside. Brody lifted her into his own arms and hurried to deposit her gently on the examining table.

"Is she your wife?"

The man shook his head, his face pale and chest moving with heavy breaths. "I found her like that, just lying on the road into town. I'm thinking she's been shot, but I can't rightly tell. She was bleeding some. Don't reckon it makes sense me finding her before the critters, what with all the blood."

Brody had already moved the light closer and saw the blood-darkened area of the dress covering her abdomen. He probed gently. "Not a gunshot. What's your name?"

"Cletus Drake, sir. I come through town

here now and again. Ain't never seen the likes of this before."

"Most people call me Doc or Brody, Mr. Drake. Sir is for fathers and politicians."

Brody recalled seeing the man a few times. A tracker, trader, and as far as Brody knew, a man who had never caused trouble in Briarwood. "You've done a good thing here, Mr. Drake. I'll need you to wait outside, if you're of a mind to stay."

"I have business with Mr. Baker at the general store when he opens, and I reckon I ought to tell . . . this town got a sheriff yet?"

Brody hovered over his patient, his eyes never moving away from his careful search around the wound. "Tom Culver, former ranch hand at Hawk's Peak. He's the sheriff now when one's needed. There was a man in jail last night for causing a commotion at the saloon, so the sheriff will be in the rooms above the jailhouse."

"I reckon then I ought to go. I didn't find nothing with her."

Brody looked away briefly to take in Cletus. A story that she'd been robbed and left for dead was plausible, if not provable. "No horse or other means of transport?" He perused her simple dress and practical boots.

"Just her. I didn't see no one else. It was too dark to search. Found her 'bout a mile east by Molly, my mule, but she could only carry the lady. I should've got her here sooner—"

"You did well, Cletus. Someone must miss her."

"I promise I didn't see nothing with her, Doc."

Brody gave his full attention for a minute over to Cletus. "I never thought you did, good man."

"It's just that some folks might think different, me being—"

"The color of your skin does not matter here. This woman owes you her life, and that is all I am thinking. Go on now and get the sheriff."

"Sure thing, Doc."

"Oh, and Mr. Drake. Thank you for bringing her into town."

The man paused at the doorway. "Will she live?"

Brody stared down at the tangled fair hair framing pale skin. "I don't know." He bolted the door when the man left and returned to the woman's side. The bleeding had stopped, thanks to Cletus, though Brody suspected she had already lost too much before the trader found her.

He spent the next hour gently removing her bloody clothes and inspecting bruises and cuts during the examination. Her corset had been no match for the blade that sliced through the thin layers. "The knife missed your organs. Good. Your recovery won't be easy, but it could have been worse." He spoke aloud to his patient, as much for her as himself. Later, he'd complete a medical chart. For now, he committed every detail to memory, first with the actions of his hand, then with his recitations.

"Bruising on one wrist, scratches on both hands. She fought someone." Brody sucked in a breath, briefly closed his eyes to pray, and examined lower. He kept his curse silent for fear she might hear him. "You're a strong lass to have fought back, to have survived." Why did they not finish the job? he wondered. Had Cletus scared them off? He could suspect the traveling trader, but a man who saves a person is rarely the same who tries to end a life.

"A single bruise along the left chin. Another next to the right eye and cheek. They will spread before they heal." He made a mental note of the herbs and medicinal powders he would prescribe, some for pain and others to help speed along the healing.

Another hour passed while Brody removed every thread transferred from her clothes into the wound by the knife. He placed precision stitches through her pale skin to close the wound. He could do nothing about her blood loss except try to replenish her fluids. The scratches and bruises he treated with ointments. The wrapping he used on her injured wrist was almost the same color as her skin.

"You've lost too much blood, lass." Brody poured fresh water from a pitcher into a washbasin and dipped the end of a clean cloth into it. With gentle care, he parted her lips and twisted the edge of the cloth until the water dropped into her mouth. To his enormous relief, her tongue moved when the water hit it. "Stay with us, lass. You've come too far to give up now."

Brody repeated the ministrations until she fell into a deeper sleep. It was a start.

2

RIVERS OF MAJESTY surrounded by mountains tall enough to soar above the clouds, and valleys so vast, one could never travel them all in a single year, spread before her. Katharine Kiely had seen much of the West, but it had always been the majestic Rocky Mountains that she yearned to explore.

This was her first foray into Montana Territory, and it had taken all her charm and considerable powers of persuasion to gain this assignment. In the end, it was a father's inability to deny his daughter that brought her to this part of the country. She wondered, though, if there had more to his acquiescing.

Katharine was not as confident that the Gallagher family of Hawk's Peak would be as easy to convince as her father. Gazing upon the expanse of meadow surrounded by hundreds, if not thousands, of trees, she tried to look at the proposal from the Gallaghers' point of view. She had never been a part of a project that sought to invade a piece of land as untouched as what lay before her.

"Miss?"

She glanced at the coach where Bessie, her maid and confidant of seven years and Stewart's younger sister, waited for her. Bessie preferred to remain in the private stagecoach they hired in Butte, for she did not enjoy what she referred to as "rough country." The man from whom they rented it owned three such decommissioned stages and appeared to delight in charging an exorbitant weekly rate. Katharine, however, was as shrewd a negotiator as her father. The supply wagon stood half-empty a few yards behind the stage.

Katharine lifted the edges of her skirts to walk the short distance back to the road through tall grass. "Oh! Oh, no—" She found her balance before her legs catapulted her forward. With eyes closed, she took another careful step forward and lifted her skirt hem out of the way. An impression from her beautiful leather boot separated what had once been a pile of something she didn't want to think about. She counted them blessed that the animal itself was nowhere to be seen.

The grimace remained on her face as she brushed her boot against the ground and tall grass. By the time she reached the coach, she was relatively certain there would be no repairing the shoe, even after a good cleaning.

She peered in through the coach window. "We won't be much longer, Bessie. It is beautiful outside, and a walk is wonderful for one's constitution."

"I am quite content sitting here, Miss Katharine . . . unless you need me."

Katharine smiled. Bessie had been with her long enough to speak her mind, but the proper way of doing things was too ingrained in the maid for her to dismiss her mistress completely. Katharine had always found her father's staff to be too rigid in their disapproval of her less formal behavior around them. It had taken her many years to show Bessie it was all right to be herself, at least when they were alone.

"I have always thought you enjoyed these adventures."

"We have never been so far from . . ." Bessie poked her head out the window, "civilization. I have heard stories of savage men and animals, and with no train or—"

"Bessie. How many times have I told you not to listen to the men's stories? They only wish to have a little fun and frighten you."

"Well, it has worked."

Katharine made a mental note to speak with their traveling companions again. They were all good men, and would do anything required to keep them safe, but the younger two—brothers three years apart in age—liked their amusements. She watched the surveyor and his two junior assistants carry their gear back to the wagon. This had been their third stop to verify the mine's calculations, and thus far, she had been unimpressed by the survey conducted by the mine owners.

"Stewart?"

Her father's head surveyor, Stewart Jaffey, a man of fifty-three years, who had sneaked her hard candy as a child, walked over.

"How does it look?"

Stewart wiped his brow with the edge of a kerchief. "Beg pardon, Miss Kiely, but it's the same as before. The measurements don't add up to what the mine gave your father."

Branson Kiely, dubbed "King of the Spur Lines," had laid track for two dozen lines of track in the West, built a successful import company in Oregon, and ruled business meetings with unimpeachable morals. He also believed in verifying everything. His refusal to move forward on a project until they confirmed land ownership, with every penny properly budgeted, is why people called upon him to see the job done right.

Katharine admired her father's business acumen and often asked herself the question: "What would Branson Kiely do?"

"Thank you, Stewart. We will settle into town, and then a meeting with Mr. Jameston from the mine is in order. I have a letter to write and then we can be on our way."

"Very good, Miss."

Stewart opened the door and helped her inside. To Katharine's surprise, Bessie climbed out.

"Stewart. We need Miss Katharine's small trunk."

In all their years with her family, Katharine never once heard Stewart question a request from Bessie. He never asked for a reason, either.

"Very good, Bessie. Give me but a

minute."

Bessie looked into the coach and directly at Katharine. "You cannot arrive in town with those boots."

The rising warmth in Katharine's cheeks lasted long enough for her maid to say, "I see everything, Miss Katharine."

She leaned against the back of the cushioned seat and released a sigh. Bessie would put her wardrobe to rights to ensure her mistress arrived in grand style, just as her father would want.

—⊰⊱—

Katharine breathed in the unfamiliar scents emanating from the quaint, one-street town of Briarwood. The usual bouquet of livestock fragrances permeated the air, and yet somehow the aroma of grass, pine, and delicious baking overpowered the hay, horses, and privies.

"Bessie, I believe we need a visit to whatever eating establishment is responsible for that wonderful smell. We can settle . . ." Katharine looked around the town with equal measures of amusement and concern. "Do you see the hotel?"

"Perhaps it is around the corner."

"Perhaps." She doubted it, though. She had hoped for a hot bath and a comfortable bed rather than more nights in the tent. The men set up a luxurious camp, but Katharine longed for a private bath in which to relax and wash away the dust from the past two days. What should have been a day's travel had become two. She considered it a necessary sacrifice to obtain the information she needed on the survey.

A boarding house at the end of the road

in front of them displayed a vacancy sign. Katharine decided she would prefer the tent rather than stay in a place near the saloon. Another cursory study of the buildings presented one large enough to possibly have accommodations, though she could see no sign from her vantage point.

"Let us look into this building here." She pointed to the large wood structure on the corner.

"If they do not have rooms, Miss Katharine?"

"Then it will be the tent for us." Katharine nodded to the boarding house. "Unless you prefer to sleep there."

Bessie shook her head and remained quiet.

"Goodness, Bessie, this is an adventure." Katharine opened the door and accepted Stewart's assistance out of the coach. She smoothed the front of her dress and stopped when she realized they'd drawn the attention of passersby. "Stewart, please assist Bessie. I will see about accommodations."

"Miss, you need not do that. I will—"

"I know, Stewart, and I thank you, but this is one thing my father never allowed me to do when traveling with him. He is not here, and so I wish to explore the town, or what there is of it." Katharine raised a delicate brown brow when she next said, "And we will not be reporting everything to Mr. Kiely, will we?"

Stewart answered with a grin. "No, Miss, I don't suppose there'd be much to tell, anyway."

Katharine nodded once, smiled, and with her parasol in hand, she allowed her wide-brimmed hat to be all the shield she needed from the sun as she walked across the dirt road. She had one foot on the first step up to the general store when Bessie spoke up behind her.

"Miss, you shouldn't be walking about alone."

"This town is not big enough for me to find myself in any trouble." Katharine twisted her torso a little to look up and down the boardwalk. People entered and exited buildings, strolled down the road, smiled at each other, or stopped for a few minutes to enjoy conversation. It appeared to be a nice and clean town of residents content to go about their quiet lives. "It is cleaner than I expected."

Bessie brushed dust from her sleeve. "The roads are made of dirt."

"You've been on many dirt roads before, Bessie, and that is not what I mean. There is no one fighting in the streets, no unfortunate smells, and the buildings all appear in excellent condition. You may as well find a reason to enjoy your time here, because we are not leaving until our business has concluded. Now, let us see what this mercantile offers." Too many thoughts preoccupied her mind at once, and Katharine missed hearing the greeting called out to her by a kind-looking older man wearing a black vest over a white shirt and a starched, white apron around his waist. "I am sorry."

He continued to smile at her and said again, "Welcome to Briarwood. How may I help you today?"

Katharine returned the warm smile. "Thank you. We will need a few supplies, though I would like to look around if you do not mind."

"I don't mind at all. The name's Loren Baker." He pointed to the window with his thumb. "Are you passing through?"

She peered out the same window and saw her coach through one pane. "We will be here through the week." She approached the storekeeper. "Might I arrange an account and pay in advance? I would like those I am traveling with to charge to it." She imagined Mr. Baker had already seen the others through his window.

"Oh, that's not a problem, Mrs. . . . ."

"Miss Kiely." Katharine offered no other information about herself or the others. It was not her intention to deceive. However, the fewer people who knew of her business in the area the better, at least until she spoke with all the concerned parties.

The store was situated in a way that gave Mr. Baker a view of most of the town. Katharine realized now that the single street rounded a bend, though she could not make out what was beyond the extensive building on the corner.

"Does the building there, just across the way, have rooms to rent? We were told there was lodging in town."

"That's Doc Brody's clinic. I reckon you've seen the boarding house. It's a nice place on the inside but can get a little noisy at night on account of the saloon. I've rooms to rent upstairs. They might not be what you're looking for, but they're clean."

Given the present options, Katharine was inclined to take the storekeeper up on his offer. "How many rooms?"

"Four, and all empty."

She hoped the vacancy was not an indication of the rooms' comforts. Her attention, and Mr. Baker's, temporarily shifted when a woman about the storekeeper's age approached carrying three empty baskets.

"This is my wife, Joanna."

The neat-as-a-pin woman with bright and gentle eyes decided it for Katharine. "It is a pleasure to meet you, Mrs. Baker. We will take the rooms for one week, if they will be available."

"All four?"

"Yes, please. I will pay in advance if that is a concern."

"Not at all." Mr. Baker held out his hand and Katharine accepted the delayed gesture. How could she not when presented with such an enthusiastic grin?

She started her browsing near a basket of soaps and wondered if Mr. Baker's rooms had hot and cold running water. Bessie appeared preoccupied with an assortment of parasols. Katharine counted it a minor victory, even as she puzzled over whether she should send Bessie back to Oregon until her business in Montana concluded.

The subtle jingle of a bell announced the entry of a new arrival, and the storekeeper's boisterous greeting confirmed it. When Mr. Baker's voice shifted from jovial to solemn, Katharine looked toward the front of the store. A tall man, broad through the shoulders and chest, stood with his back to her. His thick hair of deepest, darkest brown curled at the edges and appeared almost unruly. He was without a hat or coat, leading Katharine to suppose his visit to the store required a quick journey from another part of town.

It was his voice that intrigued her most, and the pensive expression Mr. Baker wore told her the conversation was not a pleasant one. Something about the man drew her away from the shelf with various ladies' accoutrements to a table of blankets. She believed listening in on a conversation to which one was not invited showed a level of rudeness she did not think herself capable, and yet she made an exception this time.

"You've heard nothing about a missing woman?"

Mr. Baker shook his head. "It sure is a shame. Is she going to make it, Doc?"

"She's survived the night, so I am hopeful."

"Tom'll know what to do. So will Ramsey. He's found missing folks before."

Katharine tried to follow the conversation and store each name in her memory. She watched the doctor shift his weight, his discomfort about discussing a patient apparent.

"Joanna said the new bandages were ready."

The storekeeper nodded. "She wrapped them all up for you." Mr. Baker disappeared into a back room and returned a few minutes later with a large bundle. "More than usual."

"There has been an influx of accidents at the mine."

Katharine leaned a little closer at the mention of the mine.

The storekeeper passed the bundle to the doctor, and Mr. Baker made a note in a logbook. "Don't they have a doctor up there?"

"They did. He left two weeks ago."

"Makes no sense. That's always been a safe place for the miners."

"Not any longer, it seems." The doctor started for the door, but Mr. Baker stopped him with one more question.

"You tell Ethan about the doctor leaving the mine?"

The taller man nodded. "As soon as I heard. Thanks, Loren. Please keep the bandage orders steady and in the same quantity for the time being." He stood below the threshold with one foot outside and stared at Katharine.

She did not know who recognized whom first or even how. Twenty years changed people, and yet she remembered the deep, gray eyes as though she gazed into them yesterday.

"Kate?"

3

HE SPOKE BARELY above a whisper, and yet, he may as well have shouted with as clear as her name sounded on his lips.

"Miss?"

Katharine remembered they weren't alone and had in fact drawn the attention of everyone in the store, which was thankfully only a few. No one could ignore either of them: he with his imposing size and she in clothes incongruous to her surroundings.

"It is all right, Bessie. The doctor and I are—"

"Doc!"

An older boy stood in the street outside the clinic, shouting, "Anyone seen Doc?"

Without another glance in her direction, Brody dropped his bundle on the counter and ran from the store. Those inside moved closer to the windows. Katharine paid little attention to the others. She watched Brody run and meet the boy. During what seemed like only a few seconds, the doctor ran into his clinic, emerged carrying a medical bag, and with surprising speed and agility, swung up onto the back of a beautiful chestnut horse with a pattern of white. The boy untied the horse and heaved himself into the saddle atop a sprightly piebald.

Dust filled the air behind them.

"That doesn't happen too often."

Katharine regarded the storekeeper. "Pardon?"

"Rushing off like that. Haven't seen him

in such a hurry since a tree landed on Bill Landry, oh, six months ago."

"A tree just fell on this man?"

"No, Bill cut it down himself. Miracle that Doc saved the leg."

On the many site visits she made with her father over the years, Katharine had never spent time among the people in any of the towns. They visited the mines, she listened in on meetings, usually acting more like a secretary, and once finished, they returned to the closest hotel and departed for home soon after.

Before she left Oregon, Katharine had promised herself this time she would experience more. She respected the way her father conducted business, but she also believed that they could not truly make a difference until they learned about the people who would be affected by the spur lines.

"Will they need help?" She was not oblivious to the horrible circumstances that could befall a miner or railroad worker, yet she had seen nothing her father did not wish her to see.

Mr. Baker shook his head. "Doc would have said. He'll send word if he needs more men. Folks around are always willing to help."

With as curious as the people in Briarwood appeared to be about the goings-on, she was not surprised. "The doctor rode east, did he not? What is in that direction?"

Mr. Baker moved the bundle to another counter before moving back to look out the window. "Lots out that way. Hawk's Peak, a few small farms and homesteaders, and one road to the mine. There's a lot of wilderness beyond and between, too. Now that I think on it, that boy was Jimmy Derkins. His ma is due to give birth. Shame if something went wrong. Jimmy's cousin to young Levi Gibbs who works out at the ranch."

Katharine marveled at the way the man's mind shifted from one subject to the next. "What is Hawk's Peak?"

"Just about everyone in the territory knows the big ranch owned by the Gallagher family."

Katharine wondered why the mine owner omitted that bit of information regarding the land or why it wasn't in the reports provided to her father. It would make the Gallaghers easier to locate. Her entire reason for coming here lay north of town, and yet, her thoughts rested with the man she had not seen since she was ten years old and a dreamer with braids.

Her thoughts drifted back to what Brody had said about the mine accidents and the lack of a physician. She searched out Bessie, who had returned to examining the fabric, finding them more interesting than the situation outside.

"Bessie?"

"Miss?"

"I find I am no longer of a mind for shopping. You stay here. I am going for a walk."

Bessie dropped the fabric she'd been holding onto the table. "You can't walk alone. Your father wouldn't like it."

"My father would understand." To Mr. Baker she said, "Will you please show Bessie the rooms when it is convenient? I will return soon."

Katharine exited the store before Bessie tried to make her case again. She wanted to be alone as she did her best thinking in solitude. A quiet bluff overlooking the sea served as her special place at home, a spot she always thought belonged only to her and her mother.

Thousands, if not millions, of acres of wilderness surrounded her, and she had not yet enjoyed a moment entirely to herself. The novelty of her arrival had yet to wear off. A few passersby glanced her way, but most went about their business. She expected a lively town based on reports, yet it still was peaceful, even with all the activity. Patrons entered various establishments—though few in number—along the main street.

The loud clank of steel on steel drifted from the blacksmith's shop. The sheriff stood in front of the jail speaking with two men who occasionally nodded. Tantalizing aromas and conversation carried from the café she had seen earlier. The lack of noise coming from the saloon, even so early in the day, surprised her, and she made a mental note to ask Mr. Baker about it.

As she passed Doctor Brody's clinic and a large empty section of land at the end of the street, she was most curious about two things: why was there no hotel, and why did the Gallaghers so vehemently oppose a spur line? True, it was meant to go to the mine, but even a town like Briarwood, with a small population, could benefit.

"Miss Kiely?"

She turned at the sound of the familiar voice. "Stewart, you have known me since I was a girl. Can you not call me Katharine?"

"Your father wouldn't like it."

Katharine was annoyed with the phrase, especially after hearing it twice in such a brief span. She understood her father's expectations for servants, though she did not agree the rules should apply to those she held in regard and who had been loyal for so many years. It was only Bessie who used her Christian name, but she still refused to drop the "Miss." "My father isn't here."

Stewart shook his head and Katharine did not press him. "Have you sent word to Mr. Jameston?"

"I did. The telegraph runs up to the mine, and he sent a reply right back. He's got business to handle and says he'll be down tomorrow."

"Business, is it? For a man who has been so eager for our arrival and my father's help, I find this delay confounding. Please wire Mr. Jameston back and inform him that if he does not meet us as scheduled this afternoon, then our business with him will go no further."

Stewart rubbed his jaw with a gloved hand. "That's a lot of words for one telegram."

"I trust you to use words he will understand. Where are the boys?"

"Archie and Otto are taking care of the equipment, then they'll get the bags up to the rooms."

"Did you speak with Bessie?"

"I did, just a spell ago."

Katharine pulled the drawstring open on her reticule and removed the polished, silver-and-pearl pocket watch from within. "I did not realize the time. Please see to that telegram." She murmured the last as she thought of the hour that had passed since Brody rode off.

Before Stewart left her side, he said, "Your father would do the same thing, you know, about Mr. Jameston." He smiled and walked in the direction of the telegraph office, a small building near the clinic, and disappeared inside.

Katharine smiled back until her eyes focused on the sign hanging above the clinic door. She knew she was not mistaken in recognizing him, for he had whispered her name, as she did his now. "Finnegan Brody," though she saw no sign of his given name on the sign. The young man who had stolen her heart twenty years ago was now a man full grown. She was not surprised he had become a doctor, for he had spoken of little else during the time she knew him. However, she never imagined him in a small town in the western territories.

"Miss Katharine?"

She shook fanciful memories from her thoughts. "Bessie. Did you conclude your shopping?"

"I did, and Mr. Baker showed me the rooms where we will stay. They appear clean and comfortable."

Katharine heard the hesitation in Bessie's voice. "There's more."

"They do not have running water."

Her hopes for a warm bath now quashed, Katharine presented a smile. "We have stayed in more rustic accommodations. It would be far worse if we had to sleep in the tent. I do not imagine any establishment here has such a luxury."

"Mr. Baker said only the medical clinic and a place called Hawk's Peak have running water. Miss Katharine, I will not be sorry to see the last of this place when we leave."

Katharine was uncertain she shared Bessie's desire to hurry away but kept her own council for now. Her maid had proved many times that she did not possess a robust constitution.

"Come, we shall enjoy a repast in the . .

." Katharine peered at the sign as they approached the building. "Ah, Tilly's Café. Delightful." She listened politely as Bessie shared her thoughts on the fine selection of fabrics in the mercantile. She praised Mrs. Baker for her keen eye and even for selecting a hat she thought Katharine might like to try.

When Katharine led them to the door, Bessie stalled. "We can't be eating together in public. Your father—"

"Wouldn't approve. You and Stewart will need to rid that phrase from your vocabulary while we are here. Now, I do not believe you will find anyone in this town who cares about such things."

They drew the attention of most of the café's patrons for a few seconds. Some whispered, but most returned to their own conversations. Once they were seated, a young girl came to their table and introduced herself as Cora. "We have chicken with dumplings or meat loaf, if you're wantin' lunch. Apple-cherry pie if you're wantin' something sweet."

Katharine lacked an appetite for anything more than pie, but she knew Bessie had not eaten since breakfast, and one occasion in Colorado reminded her Bessie did not like meat loaf. "The dumplings for my friend, please, two slices of pie, and tea for us both if you have it."

"We do, ma'am." She eyed both women with curiosity before returning to the kitchen.

"There, you see. No one cares."

Bessie shook her head and smoothed the edge of the tablecloth. "Some people will care, Miss Katharine."

She supposed her maid was right, but for this moment, Katharine did not care about those people. Cora returned not five minutes later with a tray carrying a bowl of the chicken with dumplings, two slices of pie, and a tea service. Katharine was too clumsy to attempt a similar feat if given the opportunity. The scent of mint from the tea mingled with the sweet aroma from the pie. She stifled a smile at the wide-eyed look Bessie gave at the large helpings.

"Cora, might you know if there is a land office in town?"

Cora's perplexed look gave Katharine the answer. "Never mind. Thank you and please tell Tilly the food looks and smells wonderful."

"You know Tilly, ma'am?"

"Only by the name on her sign."

A rosy hue adorned Cora's cheeks. "I'll tell her. Will you be stayin' in town long or just passin' through? Tilly always does up a nice meal on Sundays after church, real special like."

"I suppose we look like tourists."

Cora gave their clothes a once over and said nothing. Katharine was quiet also and then studied the room. Tilly's patrons exuded a rustic charm and simplicity Katharine envied.

"We will be here come Sunday." Katharine did not make a promise to visit the café and instead left the comment open to interpretation. Katharine never tasted a better dessert and planned to coax the sweet apple-cherry pie recipe from the café proprietor for her father's chef.

After their meal, and at Katharine's urging, they walked the length and width of the town, which did not take long, and concluded their stroll in front of the empty land across from the clinic. Katharine had done her best to keep too many thoughts of Brody at bay. She was here on her father's business and nothing else.

"You know him?" Bessie pointed to the clinic.

"I *knew* him a long time ago when I was a girl of ten, before my father moved us to Oregon."

"After your mother—"

"Yes." Katharine looked up at the sun and then consulted her watch. She expected to hear from Stewart about the mine owner's reply, yet there was no sign of the surveyor. "Bessie. Why do you not go to the room and rest? I know you are out of sorts when we travel and there is little for you to attend to right now."

"I can't rest unless you do, Miss Katharine."

"Please, consider this a holiday."

"I do not think—"

"Very well, then I will make it an order. Please rest, Bessie. I will see you before dinner."

"Where will you go, Miss?"

"I shall walk. Not far," she quickly added for the maid's benefit.

Bessie wanted to argue, but with the recommendation changed to an order, she did not. However, she did cast a disapproving look at Katharine before she walked toward the general store.

Once Bessie was inside, Katharine returned to the livery where the coach, wagon, and horses were being look after. "Hello?"

The forge was at rest and the burly, balding man she saw upon their arrival was nowhere to be seen.

"Can I help you, ma'am?"

Katharine stumbled a little when she took a step in the opposite direction of the voice. When she faced the newcomer, it was with some relief. "Good day, Sheriff." I was in search of the blacksmith. Mr.

Lincoln, I believe."

"That's him. I just left Otis at the jail. He's fixing a hinge for me. If it's urgent—"

"No, not urgent. I do not wish to interrupt his work. Perhaps you might answer a few questions, if you have time."

"Will if I can, Miss Kiely."

Katharine scrutinized the man from the felt hat covering light-brown hair to the worn, but good-quality boots. However, it was the lack of guile in his eyes that told her she could trust him. Years around the people her father often did business with taught her to read a person well. "We have not met."

"No, ma'am. Name's Tom Culver. I make a habit of knowing the names of any newcomers."

"I suppose Mr. Baker and Cora told you enough to assuage any apprehension. I am not here to cause difficulty."

The edge of the sheriff's mouth inched up a few degrees. "No, ma'am. It was the lack of what they said that was telling. How can I be of service?"

Katharine did not know what to make of the man, but right now she wanted information. "How far is the mine by wagon?"

Surprise registered in his expression. "A couple of hours, depending on what the wagon is hauling."

"And by horse?"

"Half that time."

The inflection in his voice indicated a heightened interest. Katharine left the subject of the mine open, for she was not yet ready for everyone to know the purpose of her visit. Her father had taught her to learn as much as possible before revealing anything in return.

"Is there a land office in town?" Mr.

Jameston had been ambiguous about the status of such an establishment, and Cora's confusion when she asked did not leave her with much hope.

"There is on the other side of the trees next to the clinic, but with no one to run it at present. Mr. Collins moved to Denver last month. Are you looking to buy land, Miss Kiely?"

"Research. If I have a question about any land, who might be able to assist me?" She heard a movement coming from inside the livery and wondered if the blacksmith had returned unnoticed.

"Orin Floyd. He's the telegraph operator and can find whatever you need. He's looking after things until we get a replacement for Mr. Collins."

"Thank you for your help, Sheriff Culver."

She transferred her attention to the

blacksmith who was now working to bring his forge back to life. "Mr. Lincoln?"

He adjusted the wool cap on his head and made a quick study of her face. "Miss Kiely, I have your coach, wagon, and horses all taken care of."

"Thank you, Mr. Lincoln."

"Otis, ma'am."

"Thank you, Otis. I would like the wagon hitched up again, if it would not be a bother."

"No bother, ma'am."

"Thank you, and one more thing. I need directions to Hawk's Peak."

4

TOO SURPRISED TO offer any kind of protest about a woman driving out alone in unfamiliar territory, Otis gave her an odd look and went to prepare the wagon for her. No doubt he expected one of the men traveling with her to drive, and under any other circumstances, Stewart would go with her.

She believed strongly in the need to speak with the Gallaghers alone. The sheriff, however, did not hesitate to ask her plans.

"I have driven a wagon before, Sheriff Culver. I assure you I will be all right."

"Maybe so, Miss Kiely, but I wouldn't be

doing my job if I let a woman go out on her own. It's a safe stretch between here and the ranch, but it's easy enough to get lost or for something to happen to the horses. One of those men going with you?"

"Thank you for your concern, but I am not going to the ranch. Might there be someone in town who could deliver a letter to the Gallagher family ranch for me?"

Apparently confused, Tom pointed in the general direction of a house near the end of the street. "Jackson Stints is in town right now. He works at the ranch and will take a letter back out for you."

"Miss Kiely!"

Frustrated at the interruption, Katharine looked over her shoulder. Annoyance shifted to a genuine pleasure when she saw the storekeeper's wife approach. One could not look upon the smiling woman with kind eyes and not respond in kind. "Mrs. Baker."

"Joanna, please. Good day to you, Tom."

"Joanna." Tom tipped his hat. "I can see Jackson gets the letter when you're ready, Miss Kiely."

She reached into her reticule and removed the letter she had penned the morning before their arrival in town. The sheriff accepted it, and rather than wait to continue the conversation, he walked away.

Katharine watched until he entered the jailhouse.

"Is something wrong?"

She smiled at Joanna. "Not at all. Your sheriff is a curious man. I cannot decide if he wants me here or not."

"Don't worry yourself over Tom. He used to be one of the ranch hands out at Hawk's Peak and is a mite protective of the family.

We all are, really. They've done a lot for this town. Tom's been a good sheriff for us. Not much happens in Briarwood, but folks passing through behave themselves more knowing we have someone wearing a badge all the time."

Manners prevented Katharine from asking why he left the ranch. "I did not have a chance to properly thank you for your help earlier. Bessie praised your selection of fabrics and keen eye for fashion."

"Posh. I enjoyed helping her. We rarely get ladies like yourself passing through our town. We stock those items mostly for the women out at the ranch. Ladies in town like something special for weddings and christenings and such." Joanna carried a full basket with its contents hidden beneath a white cloth. She shifted the weight before asking, "Will you walk with me?"

Katharine estimated she had a few minutes before the wagon would be ready and fell into step beside the woman. "If you will allow me to help." She held out her arms to accept Joanna's basket, and the older woman readily handed it over.

"Thank you, dear. I'm going to the clinic."

"Has the doctor returned?"

"Not yet." Joanna skirted a mess left behind by a horse. "He has no nurse, and I did a bit of nursing in the war. When he has to leave in a hurry, I look in."

Katharine speculated the woman to be about fifty years, which meant she would have been a young nurse during the war. She admired her even more for it. An old injury had prevented her father from fighting, which made it possible for him to build his business and move his young family to Oregon after he established himself as an importer in Georgia.

"I hope the patient is on the mend."

"Doc Brody worked on her most of the night. The poor man hasn't slept in a full day or more."

"You look a bit pale yourself."

"I inherited it from my grandmother. Always pale, she was."

Katharine would have disagreed, but she did not know the woman, so perhaps the rosy cheeks from earlier were unusual. She thought of Brody out there now, with so little sleep and working on another patient. Perhaps he was at the mine? She found it curious that the physician employed by the mining company should leave. According to Mr. Jameston, all his employees were highly compensated. One of his greatest arguments about bringing in a spur line was he could save time and money with delivery of ore and equipment, thereby increasing wages.

Katharine supported the basket with one arm and reached out to steady Joanna when she tripped on the first step. "Are you all right?"

"Of course."

"For a moment there you looked as though you were going to faint." She helped her up the two steps to the long, open porch. "May I be of help with the patient?"

"Oh, no dear, but thank you. Doc would say I need to eat and sleep more. He's always getting on me about taking better care of myself. I saw his patient early this morning when Doc first finished up, and . . . well, it's not a sight for you." Joanna patted Katharine's hand as she might a child's. "Thank you for walking with me." Joanna entered the clinic using a key.

Katharine had not noticed earlier if Brody
had locked the door when he left in a rush.
Her gaze drifted upward to the second
level. What happened to the woman inside
to have put such a grim weariness in
Joanna's eyes?

When she returned to the livery, she was
met with another disapproving look. This
time from Stewart. She shook her head
when he would have spoken. Otis stood
close enough to overhear, and her
business in Briarwood needed to remain
quiet until she'd spoken with Ethan
Gallagher.

Stewart stumbled over the first part of
his greeting and spoke her name. There
was no choice now except to have him join
her. Without either of them speaking,
Stewart assisted her onto the wagon seat
and climbed up to fill the space.

When they were safely away from

listening ears, Katharine explained. "I can guess what you are thinking, Stewart, and yes, I intended to go out alone, and no, I was not going to the ranch or the mine. Did Mr. Jameston reply?"

"No, Miss Katharine."

"Curious that he should desperately want us here." Even as Katharine said the words aloud, she wondered if perhaps Mr. Jameston did not take her seriously because she was not her father. Would he treat a man the same way? "When we return, please wire my father to let him know we have arrived and that a letter will be forthcoming."

"A letter won't reach him before we leave Briarwood, Miss. If you're serious about not working with Mr. Jameston anymore, there's no reason for us to stay on."

Katharine studied the vast landscape as it appeared to move with every rotation of the wagon wheel. "There is reason, Stewart. We will not be leaving right away."

Stewart made no comment to that but asked, "Where are we going, Miss, if not the mine or ranch?"

She smiled at the sight of a small herd of elk traversing across an open meadow toward a wide expanse of trees. Beyond the open valley and acres of trees, hills rolled and mountains jutted above the earth. Katharine wondered how often Stewart looked through his transit and measured points of land but never truly saw beyond the angles and measurements. "We are admiring, Stewart. This land is glorious, is it not?"

Stewart moved his head back and forth to look in every direction. "It's fair enough."

No, she thought, he did not see it.

5

VIBRANT SHADES OF orange and red spread across the sky as they returned to town. The streets lacked signs of life and most establishments now rested in early darkness, with lamps sporadically glowing in windows. What voices they heard likely emitted from the saloon and café.

Guilt flashed and faded as she thought of Bessie and the brothers. It had not been her intention to remain out for so long, and it was almost time for supper. "Once you return the wagon, please see to it you and the others have your meal. I will make arrangements at the café so you may charge to an account. Bessie must be fraught."

Stewart smiled in amusement. "You are her employer, Miss Katharine. It is her job to see to your comfort, not the opposite."

"I realize you have never approved of—"

The first scream wrenched through the air. Katharine shook as a chill overcame her entire body and implanted fear in her mind. She regained her bearings quickly enough to follow the sound of the next scream to the second level of the medical clinic. "Stop, Stewart!"

She lifted her skirts and awkwardly descended without assistance. "Hurry, get help!"

"You can't go in there yourself, Miss!" Stewart reached the door before she did.

"Yes, I can." Katharine turned the knob. The door opened without a creak or moan. "Get help. Find Mrs. Baker at the General Store. Hurry!"

She tripped on a middle step in her rush

to the reach the top. "Oh!" Her eyelids pressed together as tears pooled beneath. She remained still long enough to rub her knee where it had connected with the edge of the step. Only when she could see again through the pain did she finish her climb.

The screams mellowed to sobs and led her to a room at the far end of the hallway. Katharine pushed in and paused for a moment at the sight of the thrashing young woman lying on the bed. "It's all right." She hurried to the woman's side, only to realize her eyes remained shut and her nightgown clung from sweat. One of the woman's hands connected with the headboard and still she did not awaken. "Dear, God. What do I do? What do I do?" She chanted the question to God, to the woman, and to herself as instinct took over.

"You are safe." She moved closer and

touched the edge of an arm as it swung in the air. "You are safe. No one is here to hurt you." Katharine's touch lingered longer this time. "You are safe." Her fingers caught and circled the woman's wrist before she could hit it against the small table next to the bed. She immediately released the wrist when the woman cried out. "No one will hurt you."

Katharine continued to speak soothing words as she gently touched an arm, a leg, and finally the woman's damp brow. "Hush now. You can sleep." The thrashing eased and sobs gentled to soft whimpers. "There now."

"Good heavens!" Joanna burst through the door with surprising swiftness. "I left only for a few minutes. What happened?"

"It was a nightmare. We heard her screams from outside when we returned." Katharine heard a crunch beneath her boot and looked down. She had not noticed the broken lamp upon her arrival or the pool of oil seeping into the floorboards. "Is there another lamp?"

Joanna nodded and brought one over from atop a dresser in the corner of the room. She lit the burner with shaky hands before replacing the glass chimney on the base. Light illuminated the darkening room and cast shadows on the walls.

Tears, this time of sorrow, filled Katharine's eyes. The flickering light passed over the young woman's face to reveal the trauma she had suffered. Katharine did not need to ask what happened to the poor woman, for the evidence splayed across her face in bruises and stitched wounds.

"Where is Doctor Brody?"

Joanna held the patient's hand while she looked at Katharine. "He sent word that he's been delayed. He wouldn't have left her . . . whatever he is doing . . ."

"I understand." Katharine could not grasp how one man cared for so many people on his own. "Is what happened to her . . . does this happen often around here?"

"No. It has been many years since—"

She covered Joanna's free hand with her own and squeezed. "Please forget I asked. You have been with her all day, haven't you?"

Joanna nodded. "She has slept. Not a word or sound until now."

"Go home and sleep now." Katharine removed the pins from her hat and hung it on a hook near the door. She unbuttoned her tweed jacket and hung it next to her hat. "Is this apron yours?"

Joanna watched with confusion and shook her head. "Doc has them all about the place."

Katharine slipped into the apron so it covered her blouse and skirt and tightened it around her middle. "You should go home now, Joanna. I will stay with her."

"Would you know what to do?"

"If there is difficulty before the doctor returns, I will send for you. I promise."

Joanna peered down at the patient, then back up at Katharine. "Thank you, child."

"You shouldn't work so hard, Joanna."

"Oh, my dear. This isn't work. Helping Doc Brody isn't about helping the doctor." Joanna brushed a hand across the patient's cheek. "You know, had my eldest daughter lived beyond her fifth year, she would be this young woman's age."

The pain Katharine witnessed in Joanna's eyes reminded her of all the times she looked in the mirror after her mother passed. She wondered if Joanna realized, or simply ignored, the toll tending the patient had taken on her.

"Do you know her name?"

"I know everyone in this town and a way beyond, too. I've never seen her before." Joanna left the room with less fervor than she entered.

Katharine returned her attention to the woman now lying peacefully on the bed. She drew up the blankets the patient had kicked away in the fit of her nightmare. A quick search of the room showed her fresh towels in the top dresser drawer and a pitcher of clean water set in a large porcelain bowl. She soaked up the spilled oil with three of the towels and picked up every shard of glass she could see. Katharine then poured water into the bowl and carried it with a few more small cloths to the bed.

The drip of droplets wrung from the

cloth back into the water was the only sound in the room until Katharine pressed the towel against the woman's skin. Soft sighs escaped parched lips, and she continued her ministrations until the patient's chest rose and fell in steady breaths.

"Kate?" Brody brushed a finger over the top of her hand. Pale lids opened to reveal eyes the color of warm honey.

"Finn?"

"Aye, it's me. Only you and my mum call me that. In all the towns in all the territories, what fate brought you here?"

She fluttered her eyes a few times as she cast away sleep. "How long have I been asleep?"

"It's a quarter past one o'clock in the

morning." Brody sat back on his heels and waited for clarity to reach her mind.

"Not too long, then. I kept waiting for her to awaken, and when she did not, I worried perhaps I—"

"You've done nothing wrong. It was a kindness for you to sit with her." He rose to his feet and stepped back so as not to tower over her. He walked around the bed to stand on the other side. "I didn't plan to be away this long."

Fully awake now, Katharine moved the chair closer to the bed. "What kept you?"

Brody pressed two fingers to his patient's wrist and silently counted. "A birthing."

"The child?"

He shook his head. "Stillborn. His mother almost followed."

"You saved her?"

Brody did not give a direct answer to the

question asked. "She'll live."

"Will she?"

He glanced at Katharine to determine who she meant and saw her gaze riveted on the patient. "Physically, yes. In cases like this, success depends more on the patient's will to carry on."

Brody returned to her side of the bed and held out a hand. "Come. You can sleep in one of the other rooms tonight."

Katharine shook her head. "I have rested."

"I will be close enough to hear her if she awakens."

It seemed to him she might argue, but after a minute more of studying the pale woman on the bed, Katharine placed her hand in his and allowed him to lead her from the room. Brody did not think she would have been so compliant were it not for exhaustion. He showed her to the room he used upstairs when he needed to be close to a patient. "You'll find what you need in the cupboard and dresser."

She looked around the tidy space, and he realized she was wrestling with a moral dilemma.

"You've taken lodgings above the Baker's store?"

"Yes."

"They won't be awake, and Joanna already knows you're here, doesn't she?"

Katharine nodded.

"Rest." He started to shut the door, but added, "I promise to wake you if anything happens."

Her shoulders visibly relaxed. "Thank you."

Brody closed the door and stood against the wall with one hand on the knob. Weariness he had not experienced since his early days as a medical student consumed him, body and mind. He closed his eyes and waited for the image of a young girl with pigtails to be replaced by a beautiful woman grown. What had Branson Kiely been thinking when he sent his only daughter into the territory alone? Brody breathed deeply, glanced at the closed door once more, and returned to his patient.

6

BRODY SPOONED THE last of the warm broth between his patient's lips and waited for her to swallow. He asked her every few minutes to open her eyes, but he knew she would not until she was ready. Brody did not begrudge her the extra time to heal and gird her mind to face the waiting demons.

He hoped Tom had found her family. He estimated her age to be early twenties, which meant she could be a mother. His examination did not go beyond repairing the damage, but he found no evidence that she had given birth. A daughter, or sister perhaps, lost from her traveling party.

"How is she?"

Brody organized the bowl, spoon, and cloth he had used to wipe his patient's mouth on a tray and carried it across the room to a low table near the door. "No difference." He allowed himself a few minutes to give Katharine a visual inspection. She looked much the same as when he left her alone five hours earlier, though her hair was mussed. He recalled the young girl again whose torn hems and scuffed shoes gave evidence of a child who enjoyed playing outdoors. He wondered if she had changed inside as much as she had out. "You could do with more sleep."

She did not immediately touch her hair or clothes, as most women would, to ensure they were tidy. She nodded instead. "Your running water has helped boost my spirits this morning. I am told it is a luxury in this town."

"This building was going to be a hotel. The man who built it came from New York and believed the area would build up with the discovery of more gold and silver. He left before finishing the interior. When the doctor here before me bought the place, he added the water tower and added the two bathing rooms. We're still lacking in some amenities. Electricity arrived in the territory a few years ago, but I suspect it will be many more years before it reaches small towns like Briarwood."

"The running water is more than I had hoped for." She secured the apron she wore the night before. "Did you sleep?"

"Enough. She's resting—"

Frantic knocking drew their attention. "An emergency?"

Brody prayed not and hurried from the room. Katharine caught up with him quickly enough to bear the full brunt of concern emanating from the man and woman standing on the other side.

"I dared to think someone had kidnapped you or worse!"

"As you can see, I am quite well, Bessie. I am sorry to have worried you. Did Stewart not explain what happened?"

"He did, Miss Katharine. Your father—"

"My father will understand."

Stewart rested a steady and stern look on Brody before facing Katharine. "There's been a telegram from Mr. Jameston, Miss. He says if you're willing, he'll be down from the mine at half past ten."

"Mr. Jameston?" Brody ignored the other two in favor of Katharine. "Is that what's brought you to Briarwood?"

He caught her slight flinch, but she did not answer him.

"Thank you, Stewart. Please reply that I will meet with him at half past noon.

Bessie, I will be along soon." Katharine gave neither a chance to argue. She closed the door, forcing Brody to let it go. "They mean well."

"Your father had sense enough to not send you entirely alone, but two servants are hardly an acceptable escort."

"There are actually two others with us. Stewart is my father's lead surveyor, and Bessie has been my maid for years now. She is also Stewart's sister. They are sufficient. Women, after all, do travel alone."

Amused with her, Brody smiled. "I know it well enough. We've plenty of ladies in the area who arrived here without kin, but I didn't know them at the time."

"Does knowing me so long ago make such a difference?"

"Fair or unfair, aye, it does." Brody pointed to the door. "Well done, to stand your ground with them, and I suspect long overdue. Do they often dictate your actions?"

"They're good people and mean well."

"I'd wager it was you who convinced your father you could make this trip without him. If you're here to meet with Jameston, I'll further wager that the man hasn't given up on building a spur line to his mine." The slight blush told Brody he won both wagers.

"Do you know Mr. Jameston?"

"Not well. I've met him a few times when I tended to some of his miners."

"Are there many accidents at the mine?"

Brody escorted her into the adjoining room where a tray with two covered dishes sat on a dining table. "When she brought by the soup for my patient, Tilly also delivered enough food over to feed us both twice over. Are you hungry?"

"I wasn't until I smelled the food."

He smiled and pulled out a chair for her. Brody then piled a plate with portions of eggs, bacon, sausage, and added two biscuits. "Should be warm enough still." He set the plate in front of her and did not speak again until he had also poured her a glass of cool water. "As to your question . . . a few accidents, though more than usual of late."

Katharine savored the first bite of the airy, scrambled eggs. "How do you know about my father's business?"

Brody admired the way one of her delicate brows raised and how her intent stare darkened the honey hue of her eyes. "We exchanged a few letters after you left South Carolina. I returned to Ireland to apprentice for a year with a doctor there. My grandfather was a tenant farmer, and the gentleman who owned the estate sponsored me through school at Oxford, and then medical school at Harvard."

"My father knew what you were doing all this time?"

Brody shook his head and chewed a bite of biscuit before responding. "We lost touch when I was at Oxford. By then he had contracted for his first spur line and opened his first shipping warehouse."

Katharine buttered one side of a roll and took a bite. Brody watched her close her eyes and enjoy the soft bread. "This is wonderful."

"Tilly keeps me from starving." Brody drank from his glass of water and sobered. "Your father shouldn't have allowed you to come without him."

"We have already established that women do travel—"

"This is different, Kate."

"You were the only one who ever called

me that. How did you recognize me? You have not changed so much, but I was only a girl of ten last you saw me."

Brody savored a slice of bacon as he studied her. "Your eyes, your hair, the way your mouth tilts up at the edge when you are trying to change the subject."

Katharine laid her fork and knife on the edge of the plate. "Very well, why is this different?"

"Half a dozen people have come here attempting to convince the Gallaghers to either sell the land or partner with them. The mine is profitable—always has been from what I've heard. A spur line would allow them to send out more ore, which would increase profits."

"Ethan Gallagher knows this?"

Brody leaned back in his chair. "You haven't spoken to him yet?"

"No. I wanted to before anyone else in

town learned of my business here, but you . . . well, you aren't just anyone. Why is the Gallagher family against the spur line? Surely the additional profits—"

"It's not about the money for them. They've never liked the mine."

"Yes, but it wouldn't just be about the mine. The line would come close enough to the town to make travel easier for residents in Briarwood."

Brody filled her water glass again. "Not everyone wants to connect to the rest of the world."

"Is that why you came here? With your education, you could have established a private medical office anywhere or worked at a prestigious hospital."

Brody set the pitcher down and returned to his meal. He thought she could do with a second helping of everything, though she had eaten only half of what he had given her. "A private practice in a large city would not afford me the time for my research, and a hospital would not welcome the use of herbs as medicine. This place allows me both time for research and access to many plants I cannot get elsewhere."

"How well do you know Mr. Jameston?"

"Not well." Brody finished his meal and stood to gather the plates. He urged her to remain seated while he cleared the table. "I know Ethan Gallagher doesn't like the man, and that is all I need to know."

"You base your opinion on the testimony of someone else?"

"Not as a practice. You will understand when you meet the family." Brody lowered the kettle on top of the stove he had lit a few hours earlier. "I need to brew up a cup of tea for my patient, and then I will take you to Hawk's Peak. You'll not want to meet with Jameston before you speak with Ethan."

"Who will sit with her? I do not believe Joanna is up to it. She seemed tired yesterday."

"Joanna works too hard, but she won't let anyone tell her so. The schoolteacher, Flora Carver, is the daughter of a surgeon. She sits with a patient when it's needed, though we don't tell Joanna."

"Joanna knows." She smiled at him. "A woman always knows."

Brody chuckled. "I suspect that's accurate enough. I've advertised for a nurse, but there's little interest in living in a place as far removed as Briarwood. One came and lasted only a fortnight. It was winter, mind you, and a harder one than most."

Brody steeped a spoonful of herbs he withdrew from a glass jar. The open cupboard revealed several jars filled with various herbs and plants. "There now. I'll check in on our patient and then fetch Flora."

7

"YOUR PEOPLE WEREN'T happy with you."

Katharine grabbed the edge of the seat as Brody navigated around a large rock. Once past it, he stopped and climbed down. She watched him roll the rock out of the way before returning to fill the space beside her.

"No, they were not happy. They take their jobs seriously."

"Their primary job or watching out for you?"

"My father would say their primary task is to see to my welfare."

"Your father would be right. You never

married?"

The abrupt topic shift required Katharine to consider her answer longer than necessary. "I was engaged once."

"What happened?"

"Our fathers did business together for many years. It was natural for us to consider marriage as we came of age."

"Did you love him?"

Katharine regarded Brody and took in the rigid posture and his austere expression. Surprised to find his reaction to asking such a question pleased her, she said, "As a sister might a brother, or dear friends. He married two years ago." She gave him the same in return. "You never married?"

His entire countenance softened. "I've not met a woman strong enough to want to live as I do, at least not any who were meant for me." Brody did not explain the cryptic response and instead the pointed to the horizon. "See the pair of hawks?"

Katharine leaned closer to him to see where he pointed. She followed his line of sight to two soaring birds. "How can you tell from here?"

"The way they fly, their size," he shrugged. "You learn to tell the birds and animals apart. The ranch is named for the hawks. Well, not that pair precisely, but there are a few nests around here. Why did your father not join you?"

"He is not well."

Brody pulled on the reins to stop the pair of mares. "Why did you not say so from the start? What's wrong with him?"

"He has a weak heart. Stewart, Bessie, and the others do not know, or I do not believe they know. He has spent twenty years caring about only two things: me and building his empire. I thought him finished with travel and tough negotiations over land and spurs, but when Mr. Jameston's lawyer contacted my father's man of business, I knew he would not allow himself to appear frail."

"He sent you instead."

"No, he did not send me."

"Kate."

She cringed a little at the way he drew out her name. The touch of brogue should have softened the rebuke she heard in his voice. It did not. "He knows I am here."

"When did you tell him?"

"When the others had already left for the train station." She faced him, and her knees brushed against his leg. "He would have come even though his doctor said his heart cannot handle another long journey. If not this time, then another. He has two other projects nearing completion."

"What promise did he gain from you?"

"I find your prior acquaintance with my father to be rather disturbing at this moment. You know him too well." Katharine faced forward again. "From home to here and back again, I would never be alone."

Brody lightly flicked the reins and urged the horses back in motion. "You're old enough to know your own mind."

"Yes, you do know my age. Thirty is beyond old enough, but I have not the heart to go against him, at least not so he knows."

Brody nodded in understanding. "Because of your mother."

"He has never truly recovered from the loss. I suppose his acquiescence is his way of acknowledging that I need not seek his permission. However, this is business, and for that I must give him the upper hand."

"Do you care so much about his

empire?"

"No." Katharine shocked herself with the quick response and decided the matter would require further thought later. "I care about his health, and I could not convince him to let well enough alone. He has his shipping enterprises in Astoria to keep him busy. He does not need to be in the spur business any longer."

"How does it work?" Brody veered the horses at a fork in the road so they continued north.

"Where does that road lead?"

"To the mine, and there's a trail that crosses the mountains, though only accessible by foot or horse."

Katharine made a note to have Stewart look into other routes leading to the mine. "How does it work, you asked? The spur lines?" She recited the process she learned from her father. "Branson Kiely is a skilled negotiator. When someone is unwilling to part with land, or there is a land dispute where a proposed spur line is to be built, my father mediates to find the most benefit for all parties. He then makes a small investment in the spur for a share of ownership in the line."

"Does he always lay tracks to a mine?"

"There have been three tracks built to mines. One spur was for a logging consortium in Oregon. Another was for a town in Colorado with great recreational opportunities. Much like in Briarwood, the residents were a fair distance from a larger city but wanted access to the main line. Since the spur itself did not generate enough of an income, my father built a small hotel."

"You know a lot about his business for not caring."

"I care about my father, and I am proud

of what he has built, but taking over his empire one day does not thrill me."

"Will you?"

Katharine felt more relaxed than she had in ages. There had never been someone she could speak with about her own dreams. Any man who tried to court her since she ended her engagement cared more for the position they would gain by association with her family's name and in her father's company. "I have not figured out how to tell him."

"Be honest with him. Your father was always a fair man."

"He is," she agreed.

"What is your calling, Kate?"

She smiled again at the use of his nickname for her. "I wish I knew."

He pointed again to the horizon, this time farther out and lower to the ground. "There ahead. Do you see the smoke?"

A thin trail of smoke stood out against the darker background of forested hills beyond the valley. "Is that the ranch?"

"Hawk's Peak." Brody encouraged the horses into their next speed. "It's grown a lot since I moved here."

It might have been mistaken for a small town of its own if Katharine did not know better. As they drove closer, the buildings took shape. A large house of wood and stone stood out from the rest. Beyond, in a grouping, a barn taller than the house spread out to cover a good bit of land. Corrals and various outbuildings stretched out from the barn. Farther in the distance, she made out what appeared to be another house.

"It is impressive."

"This isn't all of it." Brody steered the horses and wagon beneath a tall arch made of large, weathered logs. They passed under a wide sign that read: Hawk's Peak Ranch. "There's a lot of history to the story but they combined another ranch with this one. Ramsey and Eliza—she's a Gallagher—live in the house on the other spread. Gabriel Gallagher and his wife live in that house across the stream. Ben, he's the foreman, and his wife, Amanda, built a place on the first hill beyond the main house. Colton plans to build a house for his new bride when they return from Scotland."

"You know the ranch well."

"They've had their share of accidents, and we're all family around here."

Brody did not elaborate, though Katharine found she was curious. What kind of people built such a place without the security of a railroad close by? They would have to drive their cattle fifty miles to the nearest railhead. A spur track to

Briarwood, instead of the mine, could help the town grow and flourish, so why was this family against it?

Brody pulled the team and wagon to a stop next to a hitching post in front of the big house. No sooner was he on the ground ready to assist her down when two men walked toward them, with an animal that at first glance appeared more wolf than dog. Katharine scooted a few inches on the bench and gave the animal a closer study. The tip of a pink tongue hung out the side of its mouth, and it appeared to smile as it trotted alongside the men. The single bark it emitted sounded more friendly than fierce. Katharine relaxed as the taller of the two men rubbed the dog's head before it leaped up the steps, circled twice, and lay down with its front legs hanging over the top step. A woman came outside onto the front porch that ran the length of the house.

"I hope you have your speech ready."

Brody did not give Katharine a chance to ask what he meant. He lifted her down, and when both feet were steady on the hard-packed dirt, he remained close and waited for the two men to approach.

"Brody. What brings you out here? Is everything all right in town?"

"There is a matter I want to speak with you all about, but that is not the reason for my visit. I've brought someone who would like an audience. Miss Katharine Kiely, these gentlemen are Ethan and Gabriel Gallagher."

Katharine did not have to guess which name went with which man. Though they could be only a few years apart in age, the one who stood as tall and broad as Brody possessed a hardness in his eyes one gains only from great experience and responsibility. She did not doubt this one was Ethan, the eldest Gallagher. His brilliant blue eyes matched his brother's, and those same eyes now perused her face. "Good day to you, both. I am here on behalf of my father, Branson Kiely. Did you receive my letter?"

"We knew who you were, Miss Kiely, before the letter."

Katharine looked from one brother to the next. "And from whom did you hear my name?"

Gabriel answered her question. "We had a visit last week from Mr. Jameston."

8

KATHARINE SAT IN a comfortable chair next to Brody. The well-appointed room served as both a library and study. Shelves filled much of the available wall space, and books lined most of them. A large map covered one area of a wall, and it outlined parts of the territory, but from what she could tell, it was a topographical map of the immediate area. She recognized the land Stewart surveyed on their way into town.

The woman Katharine saw earlier on the front porch entered the room now, though she did not close the door behind her. No one seemed concerned about others overhearing their conversation.

"We'll have tea shortly." The woman took a seat on the chaise across from her and Brody, and from the silent, intimate look she shared with Ethan Gallagher, Katharine surmised this to be his wife. Her husband seemed to swallow up her smaller frame, and yet, Katharine thought that they fit perfectly together. Even their movements were magnetic. When one shifted, the other followed.

"Miss Kiely, this is my wife, Brenna Gallagher."

"Pleasure to meet you, Mrs. Gallagher."

"Please, it is Brenna. We are not formal here, among friends, and you are friend to our beloved Doctor Brody."

Katharine decided she liked Brenna Gallagher. "Call me Katharine." She almost said "Kate" but held back. She liked that after all this time, Brody was the only one who used the nickname.

Ethan sat next to his wife, yet somehow made her appear the one in front and in charge. Gabriel, with a smattering of faint laugh lines around his eyes, charmed her, though she doubted that was his intention. Both men proved themselves gentlemen with every look cast her way and every inflection of their voices. She had hoped the letter would smooth the way for her introduction, and she cursed Mr. Jameston for his interference. Considering her intrusion, Katharine appreciated their graciousness.

"I must apologize to your family for my unplanned arrival. I will not begin with pretenses, for you already know why I am here, though Mr. Jameston does not speak for me or my father, nor does anyone else."

Brenna's unexpected smile brightened her already brilliant green eyes. "You will find, Katharine, that my husband and his brother are fair-minded. It is Eliza's approval most people find difficult to gain."

With half smiles all around, Katharine heard the gentle chiding for what it was. With the tension cut so smoothly by Brenna, Katharine directed her question to Ethan. "What do you have against progress, Mr. Gallagher?"

His quick grin surprised her the most. It was not wide or vibrant but still genuine, for it reached his vivid blue eyes and softened the rougher lines of his handsome face. "You, Miss Kiely, are the only one who has bothered to ask that question, and if you are posing the question to me, you have done your research."

"Please, it's Katharine, and no, no research." She drew on the experience gained from years of sitting in on meetings with her father. "Mr. Jameston's lawyer provided reports, though I now question their accuracy."

"Why is that?" Gabriel leaned comfortably back in a wingback chair.

"My father has a long-standing policy of verifying information before entering any business contract. Since our arrival, we found a few discrepancies in the survey report Mr. Jameston provided."

"You've already surveyed our land?" Ethan asked.

"Not in the way you must think. Your land runs along both sides of the road leading into Briarwood. Our surveyor remained on the road. I suspect even that land is yours, and you simply allow its use, or there is an agreed-upon easement. Am I correct?"

Brenna smiled and said nothing. Ethan

nodded. "You do yourself credit. We're sitting here right now only because Brody brought you out here, which means he must trust you. Knowing in advance what you do about our feelings regarding a spur line cutting across our land, what do you hope to gain by coming all the way to Montana?"

A woman walked in carrying a tray laden with their tea. It was Gabriel who rose first and lifted the tray to lower it onto the table. The woman smiled at everyone and then left as quickly as she entered. As hostess, Brenna poured the tea and ensured that Katharine and Brody had a cup before sitting down with one for herself.

Brenna indicated the empty doorway. "That was Amanda Stuart. I apologize for her quick departure, but she is watching the children while we meet. Another time,

I will introduce you. She's a wonderful woman, and I think you will like her."

Katharine believed she would like anyone at the ranch if they were all as forthright and generous with their time as these three. She also realized then what an imposition her unexpected arrival must be for them. The men did not seem in a hurry for her to leave, and she found herself curious about the workings of the ranch and what drove these people to toil away and continue to build in the wild of Montana, far removed from what most consider civilization.

Even in her small, but growing town on the Oregon coast, the sea and numerous ships connected her to the rest of the world. What did she hope to gain? What did her father gain besides wealth and standing? She took for granted the conveniences and protections she enjoyed as his daughter.

Katharine responded to Ethan's earlier question. "I have nothing to gain."

"Except the money earned from a deal with the mine."

Katharine wished her father were here. He would have liked Ethan Gallagher. "I suspect you made inquiries about my father after Mr. Jameston's visit, so I will not explain to you his reasons or virtues when it comes to business. You have welcomed me into your home, which tells me you heard Branson Kiely to be an honest businessman."

Ethan smiled. "Go on."

"I want to understand, for no other reason than curiosity, why you are against a spur line. Never mind the mine. What about the town? Even you would benefit with saved time and expense transporting cattle."

Gabriel leaned forward on the edge of his chair. "Does the railroad come into your town, Miss Kiely?"

Katharine had the grace to blush. "No, not yet, but not for lack of effort." She stared at Gabriel as she gave the matter further thought. Her father had not joined the eager Astorians in their struggle to bring the rails to their coastal town, a matter she had not given credit or question to before now. "It will take time, but Astoria will see the railroad in this decade. We have the port, and it has served us well."

Gabriel asked, "Have you stuck around a town after tracks are laid and travel is more convenient?"

"It worries you what will happen to Briarwood and the types of people who might come here."

"That's always been our only concern,

Miss Kiely," Ethan said. "A spur line to the mine would mean the mine owns a considerable interest in the rail, regardless of the land it sits upon, and frankly, we don't trust Jameston."

Katharine considered his words and weighed her own carefully. "What if the spur did not go to the mine?"

A quick glance passed between the brothers. "I want to show you something." Ethan brushed a hand over his wife's shoulder and rose from the chaise. He crossed the room to stand in front of the map. Katharine followed while the others remained together. Ethan ran his finger along the map and outlined a section that covered nearly a third. "This is Hawk's Peak land. Cattle, horses, and crops are the lifeblood of our ranch. It thrives because we do not make foolish investments. It's not worth risking even an acre for what we feel are insignificant benefits from having the railroad run tracks through the land."

Katharine examined the map and followed the path around the ranch land to the town. "How did you come to own that stretch of land leading into Briarwood? It's rather far from the ranch."

"Our father purchased it not long after he arrived. The town owned it and they needed money to rebuild and make repairs after a hard winter, so he bought it, and everyone benefited. I don't think he ever had plans for the land, but he bought as much as he could. He believed in preservation, Miss Kiely. He bought the land to protect it from men like Jameston."

"And corporate tycoons like my father. You intend to do the same." Katharine would not fault the family for their commitment to safeguard this beautiful land. In her experience, progress did not always equate destruction, yet she accepted not everyone wanted growth and advancements. "Thank you, Mr. Gallagher, for your candor."

"It's Ethan and thank you for yours. You know we won't accept any deal that involves the mine. They keep trying, but I hope your father is their last attempt. Regardless of the financial proposal, we will not change our minds."

"I understand." Katharine offered him a smile and returned to Brenna. "Thank you for your hospitality. I wish it had been under different circumstances."

Brenna smiled. "It will be the next time you visit."

Katharine wondered what Brenna knew that she did not. She accepted her hand in a gesture of friendship and listened to

Brenna's quiet chatter as they left the house.

"You had something else to speak with us about, Brody?" Ethan asked.

"I do, though it's disturbing." He glanced from Ethan and Gabriel to Brenna. "I have a patient at my clinic, still unconscious, who was severely beaten. Her clothes were fine, and her hands indicate a woman unused to hard work. Cletus Drake said he found her on the road leading into town. Brenna or one of the other women may have heard of her."

"Tom knows?" Gabriel asked.

Brody nodded. "He didn't recognize her, and no one so far has come forward about missing a wife or daughter."

Brenna tapped Brody's arm to gain his attention. "When you say beaten—"

"Everything and worse that you might be thinking, I'm afraid."

"Oh, the poor woman." Brenna clutched a fist against her stomach. "What does she look like?"

"Fair skin and hair like Isabelle's. I guess her to be older than eighteen but younger than twenty-three. As I said, her clothes were fine."

"We would remember a woman like that around here." Brenna slipped a hand into her husband's.

Katharine watched the subtle interaction between husband and wife with interest. Neither needed to speak or see to react to the other.

"How can we help?" Brenna asked.

They navigated their way outside to the waiting horses. Brody helped Katharine onto the wagon seat and climbed up behind her. "Please, let me know if you hear anything. The lass is going to be in a lot of pain when she wakes up, and it will help if she has family close."

"Unless it was family who hurt her." All eyes shifted their focus to Katharine. She was not ready to expand on her utterance, and no one asked her to elaborate.

Brenna stood on the porch next to her husband and brother-in-law when she asked, "Will you come for luncheon on Thursday, Katharine?"

Touched by the invitation, she nodded. "I would be delighted."

"Do you ride, Miss Kiely?" Gabriel asked.

"A little."

"Good."

Gabriel set his hat on his head, walked down the steps, and headed back in the direction he and his brother had come from earlier. Katharine noticed a few more onlookers, and in the distance, the unmistakable sound of children's laughter drifted toward them.

Katharine and Brody waved their goodbyes, and it was not until they drove under the arch entrance to the ranch that Brody spoke. "You think someone in her family may have done this?"

"I should not have spoken up, and I apologize if it was out of place, though surely all of you must have thought it a possibility."

Brody shook his head. "I can't say I did. If you had seen . . . I know it happens, but this man was a monster. I hope a father, husband, or brother would kill whoever did this to her."

"If they were able."

Brody looked her way. "You're right. We don't know who hurt her and speculating is for the sheriff. Tom has probably already considered the possibility, but I'll tell him."

"Will they help?"

"You mean Ethan and Gabriel?" Brody nodded. "They always do."

Uncomfortable at the dark direction her thoughts had taken, Katharine returned to an earlier subject. "They were more welcoming than I expected, gracious even, considering the reason for my visit."

"They never turn away a good person." Brody reached behind and held her steady as the wagon wheel dipped into a narrow hole. Once they passed it and he released her, the skin remained warm where he had touched, despite the layers of clothing. "Ethan has more trouble than most with what's coming for the territory. Progress, the unwanted kind. He, and others who believe as he does, will hold it back for as long as possible."

"You refer to statehood?"

Brody shifted a little on the wood seat

until he sat as far back as possible. "There's been more and more talk of it."

"Most people welcome statehood."

"He doesn't deny the benefits it would bring, but the costs concern him more. The politicians' battles with each other have less to do with preserving the land than how opening it up can benefit them financially and others like them. Then there are the tribes. The concern is, will they get to keep their land? We have Crow, Cheyenne, Blackfeet, and more who have been here longer than any of us. They have already forced the tribes onto reservations, with broken promises by the government, but Ethan believes if he can protect as much of this land as possible, then it won't be lost to them. He'd buy more if it were feasible."

"I understand, though it has never been something I have dwelled upon. My father's business, and mine, has always been about progress." And, Katharine thought, she too often assumed others longed for the same advancements into the future.

"What's troubling you, Kate?"

"A startling realization has struck me, and one I do not wish to discuss right now, if you don't mind." She steadied herself as they passed over another rut. "You care about this place and the people."

"You sound surprised. I may not sound like a farm lad from the west counties any longer, or not too much, but pride in land and history still run deep. I think of Montana as home or a second home, at least." Brody pulled the wagon to a stop. Land spread out in all directions. "I'm not against a spur, but I respect the Gallagher's position. It is their land. A train to Briarwood would mean an influx of people, and more people mean growth, which brings additional troubles."

Katharine glanced his way. "It is already coming, Finn. A point I argued in defense of coming, and why my father agreed to the meeting with the mine, is because there has been talk of extending lines east of Helena to reach the central mining towns. The Northern Pacific already has a depot there. It would be easy to build a spur if the line connected to one of the new rail links, and there is potential for considerable profit."

Brody remained silent for several minutes. "When you speak of it, progress sounds inevitable."

"Perhaps. It may take five or ten years, maybe longer, but profit hunters will find a way to build up this territory." Katharine's thoughts returned to Astoria, and her father's disinterest in pushing for the railroad. With his connections, he could have helped, and yet, to her knowledge, he had not.

"What will you tell your father?"

"The truth." Katharine swept her arm wide as though encompassing the landscape. "I envy them and you. You have purpose and a cause worth fighting for, regardless of how it may or may not benefit you."

"You don't?"

"I used to think so. Strangely, had you asked me the same question twenty minutes ago, I would have said yes." Katharine checked the time on her lapel watch. "I am to meet with Mr. Jameston in town in an hour. Will we arrive on time?"

Brody mustered the team back in motion. "We will. I wish I could offer to join you, but I have to get back to my patient."

"Why hasn't she woken?"

"The brain is a mystery. Many physicians believe we will never know how it works."

Katharine did not like to think in terms of *never*. "What do you think?"

"I believe some aspects of the human body will always remain unknown. Sometimes even scientists need to rely on faith."

Brody drove the wagon past the divide in the road, and Katharine's gaze shifted momentarily in the mine's direction. Faith in others was something she did not possess in abundance. She trusted her father, Stewart, Bessie, and now Brody, but beyond them, she had given little thought to whom she could trust. The instinct was there when she needed it, to, as Brody said, operate on faith. She was not a scientist, but the principle applied.

"You know what you're going to say, then?"

Katharine watched the passing landscape and closed her eyes as a grass-scented breeze brushed her skin. She leaned her head back to let the sun warm her cheeks. "Yes. I know what I'm going to say."

9

THEY ARRIVED IN town to a frenzy of activity. From his place on the wagon, Brody peered through the small crowd. The huddled group now moved as one toward the clinic as he maneuvered the wagon in front of the building.

"Otis!"

The blacksmith left the group and hurried to their side. "Thank goodness, Doc. Joanna's been shot."

"Shot? How?" Brody climbed down.

"Don't know. She was standing outside the café with Tilly when it happened. No one saw anything."

Katharine grasped his arm. "I want to

help."

Brody did not have time to argue, and the stubborn glint in Katharine's eyes reminded him of the little girl who always stood resolute when a matter was of great importance to her. "All right." Brody grabbed the medical bag he carried with him whenever he was gone from the clinic for longer than a few minutes. He lifted Katharine down from the wagon with barely a glance at her face.

Two of the men in the crowd broke away. Joanna lay in their arms as though seated. Her ghostly complexion had taken on a gray pallor, and Brody stopped the men for a second to make sure Joanna was breathing steadily. The pulse beneath his fingers worried him more than her pallidness.

"Lay her on the table in the surgery room."

He followed the men inside, and once satisfied that his newest patient was as comfortable as he could make her, he ordered everyone out. When Katharine stood on the other side of the table, he remembered her request to be present.

"She looks close to death."

"Will you lock the door, please?" Brody unfastened the top four buttons of Joanna's blouse, then handed a pair of scissors to Katharine. "Cut the apron off first, then the top of her dress." He quickly washed his hands in a basin of fresh water before pressing his clean fingers to Joanna's neck. Brody then pressed the end of a stethoscope to different points of her chest.

"Why is she gray?"

"She's not getting enough oxygen. The bullet collapsed one of her lungs." Brody put the stethoscope aside and found the needle he needed to aspirate. "There is a pillow in the cupboard over there." Katharine did not hesitate. When she returned with the pillow, Brody gently lifted Joanna's head and shoulders. "Slide it under her shoulders." He lowered her back down. He then sterilized the syringe, a small tube, scalpel, and needle and poured more of the carbolic acid over his hands before threading the needle with silk thread.

"What are you—"

"Look away, Kate."

Brody inserted the needle above the third rib until he felt it penetrate the lung. He gently removed it until he heard a quiet hiss of air expel from the small hole. Using the scalpel, he created an opening only large enough for the tube and inserted it to allow air to flow through.

"Finn?"

"It's all right."

Katharine looked down at Joanna. "What happened?"

"Since a portion of her lung collapsed from the bullet, she couldn't fill her lungs properly with air." Brody pressed a clean cloth over the wound. "Are you sure you want to help?"

"I'm sure."

"Do you know how to prepare a kettle on the stove?"

Katharine shook her head. "If you tell me—"

Brody lifted one of her hands to replace his over the wound. "Keep this in place, with only enough pressure to prevent more blood loss." He wiped his hands as he crossed the room. In a few minutes he had stoked the fire, already lit in the morning, in the small stove and set a pot of fresh water on the burner to boil. He returned to Joanna's side and carefully lifted her upper body again. "Slide the pillow back out. I need her lying flat for the next part." After washing his hands, Brody poured more carbolic acid over them before taking Katharine's place.

"I don't want to use this unless she moves." Brody poured a few drops of liquid onto a clean cloth. "Hold this and only use it on my say so."

Katharine's nose scrunched involuntarily at the sweet, chemical scent. "What is it?"

"Chloroform. There are cases of especially older patients not handling the effects of the drug, so I use it only when absolutely necessary." Brody observed his patient. She breathed easier now and remained unconscious. He prayed she stayed that way as he probed the opening in her chest where the bullet entered.

"Kate, if you are uncomfortable with the sight of blood, I need you to go now, please."

Her skin went a shade paler. "I'm staying, and I'm all right."

Brody appreciated the fierce determination in her eyes and watched her as he searched for the bullet. He used his sense of touch to see his way into the wound. "It went deep enough to puncture the lung, but . . ." He located the bullet and used his fingers rather than forceps to pull it out and dropped the bloody bullet in a small bowl. His probing caused Joanna to flinch. "Hold the cloth above her nose." Brody watched as Joanna drifted a little deeper into sleep. "That's enough." He spent several minutes checking the wound for any dirt or debris the bullet may have carried with it. "The water should be at a boil now. Pour a little of the carbolic acid from the amber bottle there into the small bowl next to it. Good. Now, fill the bowl with boiling water."

Katharine followed his instructions while he finished his search of the narrow cavity to make sure nothing else had been torn or punctured. Katharine set the bowl of steaming water near him, and Brody used a syringe to draw in some water and slowly push it back out into the wound. He repeated the cleansing twice more before he was satisfied that he'd cleaned the wound the best he could. The tear in her skin required only five neat sutures to close it. Brody stood straight and stretched his back to ease the tightness in his muscles.

"Thank you, Kate."

She expelled the breath she'd been holding for the last several seconds. "How have you managed by yourself all these years?"

Brody went to the stove and poured some of the remaining hot water into another bowl and cleaned his hands. He then dumped the bloody water in a barrel outside, stacked on a cart for ease of transport. Back inside, he refilled the bowl with fresh water for Katharine. "You'll want to clean those before the blood sets."

Katharine glanced down at her hands and the light smears of blood. "I hadn't realized." She dropped her hands into the water and quickly pulled them out. The next time she tested the heat carefully and allowed her skin to get used to it before submerging them again. She used the soap Brody had left within reach.

"I've managed well enough. Joanna seemed disappointed the first time I put out an advertisement for a nurse. I think she enjoyed sitting with patients and assisting with surgeries. She would hand me instruments, boil water, or comfort a family member."

Katharine wiped her hands dry. "And I cannot even light a stove."

"You'd make a fine nurse. You did very well your first time and put Joanna's well-being before your own comfort." Brody smiled as he smoothed a thick substance over Joanna's stitched wound and covered it with gauze. "I could use some help with this part." He wrapped a long strip of gauze around Joanna's waist, handing it off to Katharine to run it under her back as Brody cradled the woman so a small gap remained between her and the table. He watched her face and noticed the signs of her coming out of the stupor. Brody held the chloroform cloth over her mouth and nose for a few seconds until she drifted off again. "She must rest a little while longer.

Once she's awake, I'll give her tea for the pain." They finished wrapping the wound, and Brody tied off the edges.

"What did you put on the stitches. It looked like—?"

"A bit of honey."

"Yes, but honey for a wound?"

He smiled. "Healers have used honey for centuries to help prevent infection. It may not be widely accepted these days, but I find healing works best when science and nature labor together."

"You won't allow her to continue helping after this, will you?"

Brody did not answer her question right away. He leaned over his patient and spoke in quiet tones. "Joanna? Rest now. You'll come back to us when you're ready."

A soft moan escaped Joanna's lips.

"Will she be all right?"

"Fit as ever in a couple of weeks. She'll

be more upset about the inconvenience than about the pain." Brody held a hand to Katharine's back and walked her into the next room. "Why do you think she shouldn't continue to help, if it's what she wants?" Katharine's gaping expression answered his question, but Brody wanted to hear her reasoning.

Katharine pointed to Joanna laid out in the surgery. "She could have died."

"She could have, but not from using her nursing skills. Joanna was at far more risk helping soldiers during the war than she is tending to folks she cares about here in Briarwood."

"Shouldn't a woman her age be more careful?"

"Careful doing what? She enjoys her work and her life. Sure, I've told her to slow down, but it hasn't done much good." Brody led her farther away, and once in the kitchen, guided her to a chair. He was not sure if she realized how much the ordeal had exhausted her. "Tea or coffee?"

"Nothing, thank you."

"Whiskey, then." Brody pulled a bottle of Jameson's from a top cupboard, along with two glasses, and poured three drams into each. He placed a glass in front of her. "Sip it only. There's not enough there to do more than warm your insides."

Katharine stared at the glass, then looked up at him. "This is what my father drinks."

"I know it." Brody grinned and sat in the chair on the other side of the table from her. "My grandfather sent me a bottle from Ireland the first year I was in America. I never learned how he managed such an expense. I gave it to your father, and he insisted we share the bottle."

Katharine swirled the amber liquid

before taking her first sip. "It is familiar." She put the glass aside and looked at Brody. "I did not know how close you and my father had become during those two years."

"You were young. By the time I was old enough to enlist, there was talk of the war ending. Your father had his injury, and I had my first apprenticeship."

"Would you have fought in the war?"

"The Irish have war coursing through our blood, and we make no apologies for it, but I was convinced healing benefited the soldiers more than an extra rifle."

Katharine took another sip. "Did you always want to be a doctor?"

Brody nodded. "Always. My family could not afford the education, so when my grandfather's landlord first made the offer, my grandfather insisted I apprentice for two years first. He wanted me to be certain."

"I should think he would have been proud for his grandson to become a physician."

Brody smiled at the memory upon first learning when what he longed to do with his life was within reach. "He was, but he could not accept the generous offer without certainty, and so I came to America to intern with an old friend of my mother's who had a small practice in Charleston." Brody left his untouched drink on the table and stood. "Finish your drink. You'll feel better. I must look in on Joanna and then speak with Loren. He'll be waiting outside."

Brody walked out of the kitchen and through the adjoining room into his surgery. Joanna was still asleep, but to his relief, her chest rose and fell with gentle breaths. He spread a blanket over her, and with as much care as possible, he lifted her into his arms and carried her upstairs and into one of the recovery rooms. Once he removed her shoes and had her tucked beneath another loose blanket, Brody looked in on his other patient.

Asleep in a chair near the bed with a sewing sampler forgotten in her lap sat Flora Carver, her shoulders slumped forward. In the bed and sitting upright with wide eyes boring into him was his patient. She clutched the sheet close to her body. Brody remained by the door. The sensation took him by surprise every time and yet never failed to touch his heart. All the hardness and pain he witnessed somehow balanced out whenever a patient lived.

"Welcome back."

10

"WHERE AM I?"

Brody marveled at her ability to articulate. The cuts he had treated around her lips no doubt pained her every time she moved them. "You're in Briarwood at the medical clinic. I am Doctor Brody." He walked a few feet into the room. "That is Fiona Carver. Do you know how long you've been awake?"

"No, I . . . I don't . . . Briarwood?" She dropped the sheet to press a fist to each side of her head.

"Don't force it." Brody moved with caution to the foot of the bed. "Your mind and body will take time to heal."

"Your voice is . . . you're a doctor?"

"I am."

"Then you . . ." She tugged the blankets close again, this time up to her chin. "What happened?"

"You don't remember?"

She shook her head in a slow, jerking pattern.

"It's all right, and probably better for now. Do you know your name?"

This time she focused on a spot beyond him before lying back down and turning her head to look out the window. "No."

"Do you feel up to eating? You've had only broth and water these past two days. More substantial fare will be good for you." Brody did a visual examination as his patient mulled over the question. The bruises around her cornflower-blue eyes and pale cheeks would change color again and fade. The purple and blue discolorations stood in alarming contrast to her pale skin. He knew from his original inspection that she possessed many more across her arms, legs, and abdomen. "What can I do for you right now?"

Flora's eyes fluttered open, and she sat up straight in the chair. Her sewing fell to the floor, and rather than retrieve it, she let it rest. "We've been frightfully worried."

The patient kept her head averted from them both. Brody held out his hand to Flora and motioned her to come away from the bed. With indecision etched on her face, she gathered her fallen sewing and exited the room.

"We'll leave you alone for now, if you want."

The young woman nodded. The sooner she made her own decisions, the better for her mental recovery.

"Would it be all right if I have Tilly bring some food over? She runs the café. You seem strong enough to eat on your own."

Again, a brief delay, and then a nod.

"Good. Good, then. We'll need to check your wounds soon, but you won't have to talk unless you want to, and until you're ready." Brody waited for her agreement and when he didn't get it, he added, "I'll have a nurse in the room."

She nodded this time and looked at him. "I sense you saved me, but I can't do this right now."

"You don't have to explain. Promise me you will call out if you need anything."

Her cheeks blossomed into a light shade of pink.

"You're not strong enough to go to the privy outside. The clinic has a bathroom upstairs, just across the hall. It might be difficult for you to walk, though. If you need—" Her expression told him she knew what he was about to say, so he changed course. "There's a chamber pot beneath the bed. I leave the choice to you."

"Doctor . . ." She searched her recent memory for his name.

"Brody."

"Yes. There was a woman who sang to me. She sounded like my mother when I was a little girl." She reached up with a scraped hand and gingerly touched a cut on her mouth. "Will she come again?"

Brody had heard Joanna and Flora enough in church to know it wasn't either of them. "I will ask her. Rest now, and food will arrive soon."

When Brody went downstairs and opened the front door to the clinic, Katharine stood on the other side of the threshold with a small group of people standing around, their mouths half open as though they all stopped speaking in mid-sentence at once. Relief softened the tense lines around Katharine's eyes and mouth.

"You all have questions about Joanna, and your concern is appreciated, but only Loren and Tom can come in right now." Brody saw Katharine's maid and the surveyor standing at the end of the porch, presumably waiting for the others to disperse so they could whisk her away.

"Katharine." He bent his head so only she could hear. "I know you have other business, but will you return later? Our patient asked for you, or rather, for the woman who sang to her. I assume she meant you."

Her already rosy cheeks blossomed. "I will return as soon as I am able."

Brody watched the gentle sway of her skirts as she walked away. A second later she returned to hand him the borrowed apron. "Did she tell you her name?"

He shook his head. "No, but it's still early days."

This time when Katharine left, she and her maid separated from the surveyor and walked directly to the general store. Brody imagined Bessie would not let her mistress go anywhere else until she was presentable. He closed the door and faced the two men. "Tom, if you'll wait in the kitchen, we'll talk in a minute. The coffee on the stove is strong and should still be hot. Loren, I'll show you to your wife now."

"Promise me she's all right, Doc."

Brody dropped a comforting hand on the aging storekeeper's shoulder. "She's alive, and I expect her to recover. She'll need a lot of rest, and we'll watch closely for infection."

It took ten minutes longer than expected

to answer all of Loren's questions, and another five minutes to assure him again that his wife would fully recover, so long as she rested for the next two weeks. When Brody returned downstairs, Tom sat at the wide table with a cup of coffee in front of him.

"How is Joanna?"

Brody poured himself a cup of the strong, dark brew and sat down across from the sheriff. "She'll make it. What happened?"

Tom leaned forward with his arms resting on the table's edge. "She was standing outside the café talking with Tilly. According to Tilly, Joanna walked away right before she heard the shot. Joanna stumbled a bit; otherwise the bullet might have hit her square in the heart. A second bullet went through the café window and would have hit one of the patrons if they hadn't all gone to the floor after the first shot."

"Who was in the café next to the window?"

"Can't find him. Tilly said it was a miner, but she didn't know his name. By the time I got to everyone, he had slipped away."

Brody leaned back in the chair and thought of Joanna. "She was in the wrong place."

Tom nodded and finished his coffee. "I'm headed out to the ranch next to speak with Ramsey. I don't have his experience, and now I've got two people here in your clinic who nearly died."

"Ramsey already knows or will soon, at least about the young woman upstairs. I said something to Ethan and Gabriel, which means—"

"One or all of them will show up to help as soon as they get organized. They can't know about Joanna yet."

Brody shook his head and carried the empty coffee cups to the sink. "Despite some unfortunate incidents over the years, Briarwood has been a peaceful refuge for folks. Now I have two women upstairs, one beloved and the other who may never recover from what happened to her. One criminal at a time is bad enough, but two—"

Tom stood and picked up his hat off the back of the chair. "Why two?"

"You think one man attacked my first patient and then shot Joanna?"

"Not necessarily." Tom held up a hand to stop Brody from speaking. "I'm also headed to the mine after I speak with Ramsey and ask Colton to lend his time."

Brody had met every ranch hand at least a few times, but he didn't know half of them beyond their injuries or the occasional hello. The other half, which included Colton, he'd come to know because they possessed abilities that were called upon repeatedly for the good of others. Colton's ability to track man or animal over any terrain and in almost any weather was well known. "Cletus Drake found the woman almost three days ago. Whoever left her there won't be waiting around for a tracker to find him."

Tom secured his hat in place and walked to the front door. "I reckon he won't, which is why I'm hoping Ramsey and Colton will have some ideas on how to find him."

"And the man who shot Joanna?" Brody opened the door and stepped outside with Tom.

"We're all doing our best, Doc."

Brody plastered on a half-smile and waved to a family walking past them. "I know. I just wish there was more I could do for my patient upstairs."

"You ever see anything like it, Doc?"

Brody waited for a pair of riders to pass his clinic before responding. "Once." He did not offer Tom more information, for even after twenty-one years, he could still see the young widow's broken and bruised body laid out on the bed, for she'd been too far gone to save her. If Brody had not vowed to become a doctor by then, that incident would have decided his course.

11

KATHARINE STOPPED AT the stream's edge where a flat rock served as a welcome place to rest. After a few minutes of silence, she admitted it was not merely rest she needed but an escape. Every aspect of her life was as clear as a cloudless sky three days ago, and now she suffocated beneath the weight of indecision. She closed her eyes and listened to water flow and lap over rocks as it traversed through the landscape, while her meeting with Jameston circulated in her thoughts.

"Our agreement is with Branson Kiely, not you."

"You have no agreement beyond our

consideration. There is no contract. First, you fail to make our original meeting, and I have learned you no longer have a physician at the mine." Katharine sat across from Jameston in the empty land office. Stewart took up the seat next to her, and Bessie remained at the general store while the others conducted their business. The land office had been the only place that offered privacy without risk of interruption. The telegraph operator kindly offered it when Stewart went in search of a location for their meeting.

"We can't make a doctor stay at the mine."

"Our directives were clear, Mr. Jameston. To gain our consideration, you guaranteed not only the survey report you provided our lawyer but also that your workers were well compensated and cared for, and proper care requires a doctor."

"Doc Brody in town tends to the miners just fine, Miss Kiely."

"Undoubtedly, but Doctor Brody's obligations are to the town. If one of your men suffers a serious injury at the mine, and Doctor Brody is unavailable or unable to reach the man—"

"That doesn't—"

"Do not interrupt me again, Mr. Jameston." Katharine thanked Stewart when he gave her a glass of water. He did not make the same offer to the other two men in the room. "Kiely Limited will not be doing business with you or your mine."

Mr. Jameston stood and leaned forward with both hands planted on the rough table. "We came to you because we were told Branson Kiely could make any spur deal happen with his connections and backers."

Katharine tapped her hand on Stewart's

arm to keep the situation diffused. "You heard correctly, Mr. Jameston, but you will not be getting our backing or the Gallagher's land."

He lifted a hand and slammed it back down. This time Stewart ignored her touch and stood to put his body half in front of her. Katharine did not even flinch.

"Do you have any idea how much money your company can make, Miss Kiely? How much the Gallaghers, and everyone else involved, can walk away with?"

Katharine lifted the glass and sipped and took her time to set it back down and stand. Her intention had been to show the odious man that he did not dictate terms or timing. She achieved her goal when Jameston pushed his chair with such force it toppled backward and skidded across the floor.

"Money, Mr. Jameston, is only one

aspect of our consideration, and in this instance, no amount of it will change my mind. Before you assume you can work around me and go to my father, know this: you will never do business with Kiely Limited."

Jameston stalked from the land office, leaving the glass in the door to rattle as it opened. The mine worker who had accompanied Jameston, and whose name his employer failed to provide, lifted the fallen chair, tipped his hat in her direction, and exited with far less noise.

Katharine watched the door to make sure neither man intended to return.

"You all right, Miss Kiely?"

"I am, Stewart, thank you." She longed to loosen her corset and breathe deeply. "Please send a telegram to my father explaining the deal with Mr. Jameston will not move forward."

"Mr. Kiely is going to ask why."

"Yes, he will." Her father would also be furious and demand Stewart drag his daughter home if he heard of all she had already been through in her short time here. She was certain Branson Kiely would not care about losing the deal. "Do not tell him anything about this meeting, Stewart. You must promise me. The telegram can simply say we could not trust the information provided. He will understand." Katharine started for the door, then stopped and added, "Also tell him he will be glad to hear I have been reacquainted with his old friend Finn Brody. A letter with details is forthcoming."

"That's an awfully long telegram."

"Please see to it." Katharine remained composed as she left the small office and walked down the dirt street, shaking her over Stewart's disdain for long telegrams.

"Miss Katharine!"

She waited for Bessie to reach her side.

"You look a fright, Miss. You ought to rest."

"No, Bessie, I wish to walk."

"We can go to the—"

"No." Katharine gentled her next words. "I need some quiet time to think. I will not venture far."

Bessie did not appear to believe her, which was understandable considering the last time she made the same promise and did not return for hours. The maid wisely kept her own counsel, though Katharine sensed the other woman watched as she walked away.

Alone now by the water, her thoughts caught up to the present. She would apologize to Bessie later for dismissing her. Bessie had been the one person in whom she could always confide her feelings until now, and Katharine agonized over what had changed since their arrival.

"I recall once a young lass who sat near the creek behind her father's house, much like you're doing now." Brody lowered himself to the grass next to the rock. "You've a lot on your mind."

"It is odd to think of myself as a little girl, and you were already a young man grown and learning the ways of the world, yet now, the years do not seem so far apart." Katharine glanced up at the rustling leaves above her. How easy it would be to stay in that spot forever. Brody resembled the man she knew long ago, at least in the way his eyes reflected the color of a stormy summer sky. His dark hair remained unruly and curled more at the edges now. She imagined he did not have time to visit the barber often. "Mr. Jameston is hiding something."

Brody took a few seconds to consider. "Hiding what?"

"I do not know, but his reaction was troubling. He makes a good profit at the mine; our lawyer verified as much before I came out here. I have been in the room when Father conducts business. He is shrewd and firm and has sent many men away from his offices, but never have I seen one behave as Mr. Jameston did today." She smiled then and looked at Brody. "How are your patients?"

"Joanna awakened and went back to sleep soon after. She needs the rest. Loren hasn't left her side. Our young woman without a name asked for you again."

Katharine planted her feet on the soft earth and scooted to the edge of the rock. "How is she?"

"She remembers nothing yet, or if she does, she would rather not speak of it, which I expected. Your singing reminded her of her mother." Brody got to his feet and held out a hand for Katharine. "I could do with a walk before I return. Will you join me around the meadow?"

Katharine accepted his assistance, and once standing, brushed her plaid skirt and fell into step beside him. She considered herself a tall woman by most standards, but next to Brody she felt like the delicate child who used to follow him around her father's house. "What will happen to her now?"

"She'll stay here until she's mended." Brody stopped so Katharine could cross the small footbridge ahead of him. "Finding the man who hurt her will not be easy. I doubt he's still in the territory."

"What about whoever shot Joanna?"

"Joanna wasn't the intended victim. A man from the mine was inside the café, right behind where Joanna stood. According to Tilly, Joanna moved before she heard the shot. If she hadn't, she may not have made it. A second shot went through the window."

Cheerful shouts came from children running into the meadow. One of the boys pulled a kite behind him as the others chased. "What happened to the young woman and Joanna contradicts the safe town I've seen so far, where parents allow their children to play unattended. Do they not worry?"

"It is different here. Boys and girls their age are used to running about alone. For all its beauty, this can be a hard and unforgiving place. Folks teach their young ones early to be cautious, but they don't live in fear."

Katharine considered the differences in her own upbringing. Her father had kept her protected and relatively unaware of the tumultuous war, though sometimes she saw smoke marring the faded blue sky. She recalled how different her father had become when the war ended, with his relief replaced by despair when her mother became sick. A poor constitution, the doctor had said.

She wondered now if her mother would have lived had Finn been a doctor then, with the knowledge he now possessed. Her memories over the following years spread one into the next and kept her young mind so enthralled, she rarely had time to think of the mother she had lost.

Once Branson Kiely set his mind to an idea, he stopped at nothing to see the plan come to fruition. He decided the great Pacific northwest held their future. Rather than travel by land, her father had sold everything except clothes, essentials, and a few precious keepsakes belonging to her mother. They embarked on a steamer to Panama, crossing through tropical jungles, and booked passage on a ship north where he built a new empire. He never returned east.

"You've gone away."

Katharine brought her thoughts back to the present. "I was thinking of when we first arrived in Oregon. My father thought to leave all the fighting of the Civil War behind, yet when we arrived, battles raged between settlers and the local tribes. I was too young to understand, and it did not last long or come so near that we suffered its effects."

"Yet?"

She smiled at how well he was already learning her thoughts. "When my father learned of his weak heart, he ignored the doctor's warnings for almost a year. He suffered a heart attack."

"The way you speak, it sounded—"

"Oh, he is well enough, but he is lucky to be alive. Summer last, when fire swept through Astoria—our home and my father's business, save one warehouse, remained untouched—he shifted much of his focus to preserving and restoring. He has always been a kind man, but the level of philanthropy he has shown in the last several months is out of character. Who he is becoming has not caught up to me yet." A small herd of deer crossed the open valley, drawing the children's attention. "He would respect the Gallaghers' decisions and dedication. It is admirable."

"Did he already know the family did not want to use their land?"

She nodded. "Our lawyer noted it in the

report he provided."

"Then why let you come here?"
Katharine's brow creased. Bemused, she tilted her head back to look in his eyes. "You ask a smart question, Finn Brody. I suppose because he never stops building his empire." She accepted Brody's assistance over a narrow part of the creek where it had snaked around and interrupted their walking path, and Katharine realized now how far they had walked from the center of town. The farther they strolled, the quieter the air, and the louder her own thoughts. "I believe there is a matter about which my father has not revealed to me, and I feel it as strongly as I believe Mr. Jameston is hiding something.

12

"DOC BRODY!" TOM sat atop his horse on the other side of the small footbridge they had crossed earlier. He held the reins of Brody's beautiful paint horse, saddled and ready to go.

"There's trouble." Brody took her hand in his and started toward the sheriff. Regardless of the possible emergency, Katharine sensed he did not want to leave her alone, even so close to town. He did not rush his steps to where she could not keep up.

He released her hand once they reached Tom. "What's happened?"

"We're not sure yet. A miner showed up

saying there's been an accident. A big one."

Brody held the reins Tom handed to him. "We would have heard a large explosion."

"I agree. The miner—name's Harry—is sitting in my office right now. Refuses to leave until I return."

"I have patients here to see to, Tom."

Katharine saw the struggle Brody waged within . . . his oath to care for all those injured against his responsibility first to the people of Briarwood. "I will check in on them."

"You're certain? They are not your responsibility, Katharine."

"I am sure. Go."

Brody pulled himself easily onto the back of his gelding, and with a long, studied look in parting, he followed the sheriff from town.

Katharine took her time to cover the rest of the distance between the meadow and town. She stopped and stood in the center of the empty area across from the clinic, closed her eyes, and allowed herself to dream of . . . possibilities.

"Miss Katharine!"

Her dreams flitted away at the sound of Bessie's voice.

"I've been watching and waiting. You promised not to go far."

How had she forgotten about Bessie? She had not thought of Bessie once during her walk with Brody, or of Stewart and the brothers. "I didn't go far. I was in the meadow all the while."

"Stewart looked for you. He is wondering, or rather, I am . . . We are curious if you have given thought to our departure now that your business has concluded."

Her business, if it still was, had not seen a satisfactory resolution. "We are not yet ready to leave, which I can see now distresses you."

"I am here to be of service as always, Miss Katharine," she said with a smile.

How long had Katharine allowed herself to believe she needed a maid to wait on her? She should have dismissed the idea when her first maid left to marry, but then her father hired Bessie, and Katharine saw her as more of a friend than a servant. Now . . . what now? "I meant what I said before, Bessie. Consider your time here a holiday."

"But Miss—"

"No argument, not this time. I have not concluded my business and may not for some days yet. I said we would stay until the end of the week, at least, and stay we will." Katharine saw the anxiety her harsh words had caused and softened the next ones a little. "Are you really so unhappy out here?"

Bessie removed a starched white handkerchief from her hidden skirt pocket, though she did no more than twist it in her fingers. "It is a godforsaken land, Miss Katharine. Do you not miss home? The sea air and . . . civilization."

Katharine did not fault Bessie her opinions, but when she looked around, she could not agree. Godforsaken? No place bearing earth's bounty with such wild abandon and beauty could ever be forsaken, by God or anyone else. "Enjoy the free time, Bessie, and we will speak again tomorrow. I have no wish to keep anyone here who does not wish to be."

The maid looked as though she wanted to say more. Instead, she bobbed her head once and walked back toward the mercantile. Katharine thought of the meadow and Tilly's Café and Otis's livery with horses for rent. She knew Bessie enjoyed riding and was more skilled than she, but apparently she did not wish to enjoy it here. Katharine had not noticed before, but did Bessie spend all her time in Loren's store?

Stewart found her as she stepped onto the long porch in front of the clinic.

"What has upset you so, Stewart?"

His lips creased into a thin line. "Mr. Jameston's been talking, Miss Kiely, about your reasons for coming here. Most folks ignored him. A few, though . . . well . . . there's mixed feelings about it."

How long had she been in the meadow with Brody? Long enough, it seemed, for the gossip to spread. "There is no help for it now, Stewart. The townspeople were bound to learn of it, and since I have now spoken with the Gallaghers and made my decision, what Mr. Jameston says does not matter."

"There's more."

There always was, she thought, and let out a sigh. "Well, what is it?"

"He's saying you plan to still build a spur, no matter what."

"Idle gossip. People will not believe it when he has been trying for years to bring the railroad to this part of the territory." A light throbbing pressed against Katharine's temples. "I have another task for you, and it must be done quietly."

"Anything you need, Miss Kiely."

"Do you remember the survey you did of the land in Utah five years ago and what you found?"

"Yes, I remember . . ." Stewart's eyes widened. "Oh."

"Exactly. I need you to do a similar

search on the land you surveyed for the spur but go a little farther north."

"Do we have permission for this survey, Miss Kiely?"

"You won't be doing a survey. Call it an exploration, and no, I did not have reason to ask the Gallaghers when I met with them. It's important, Stewart." Katharine turned the knob on the clinic door. "Where are the brothers now?"

"I've been trying to keep them busy cleaning and checking all the equipment, but there's been nothing else for them to do. They're over at the café right now."

In the normal course of business, they would either be at work already on the new project or headed to another job site. "How long will the search take you?"

"I suspect the rest of the day and maybe some tomorrow. There's a lot of land."

"Take the brothers with you. It should

not take as long with their help and will keep them busy. I trust you will find something before you have to walk the whole of it." Katharine ticked off the days in her mind. Tomorrow would be Thursday, which meant luncheon at Hawk's Peak. "We will speak after your search concludes. Please have the boys pack all the gear and ready the wagon for travel."

"We're leaving?"

Katharine did not answer him. "Please see to it and find me here when it is done." She ignored his disapproving look, entered the building, and closed the door before he left. With a deep sigh and silent question about the path she was walking, Katharine put her jacket and hat away in Brody's office, donned one of the large, clean aprons, and made a pot of tea in the kitchen.

Her father would be pleased, and she hoped, proud. The simple task was one only the cook performed at home, but for Katharine, it was an excellent step . . . to where?

She carried a tea-laden tray upstairs and delivered the first cups to Joanna, who slept, and Loren, who bless his heart, snored loudly in a chair next to his wife's bed. Katharine wondered who managed the store in his absence and made a mental note to find out if the brothers could be of some service while they were still here. They were good boys, but their exuberance exhausted her too much to have them around for long.

Two cups and a pot kept warm with a thick cloth wrapped around it, remained on the tray. She pushed open the slightly ajar door to the room where she hoped Brody's unnamed patient was resting comfortably. The young woman's feet were on the floor and she leaned the top half of her body heavily on the small bedside table.

"Mary." The harsh whisper came out as a plea.

"Is your name Mary?" Katharine hurried into the room. "Here, let me help you."

"Go away."

"It will—"

"Go away!" The words came out on a sob.

"I don't understand." She did, though, when the sharp lightning of pain struck the back of her head and coursed through her body. Her blurry eyes caught sight of a teacup shattering and another rolling across the room before everything within and without shuttered to blackness.

13

THEY REACHED THE split road where it branched into two distinct directions. West to the ranch and north to the mine. He thought all the while of his two patients who he knew were in capable hands with Katharine to watch over them, but what if something happened that required medical attention?

Brody was often called away to visit farms, but none so far away as the mine, and none requiring so much of his time of late. He would speak again with Jameston about bringing in another physician to look after the miners.

"Hold up, Brody."

He brought his horse to a stop and shifted in the saddle to look back. Two riders and their horses kicked up dust on the road from the ranch. As they drew closer, Brody recognized Ethan Gallagher with Ben Stuart, the ranch foreman.

Ethan came abreast of Brody's horse. "Colton told us what happened. He's been up around the mine searching for a sign of the man who shot Joanna and saw one of the men ride to town."

Tom asked, "He found the shooter?"

Ethan settled his black steed, who seemed more inclined to continue running. "Not yet, but he found tracks that look promising. He followed them from behind Otis's livery. Ramsey rounded up a few men who could be spared from nearby farms and ranches. They're looking for any sign of whoever attacked your patient, Doc." Ethan jutted his chin in the direction of the mine. "Let's get moving before Jameston can cover up what may be another incident."

"We haven't had proof yet, Ethan, to suggest they've been anything more than accidents. You know if we did—"

"I know, but these aren't accidents, and we're not letting it rest this time until we find proof or someone who will talk." Ethan's horse decided on who would lead the way. The others fell in behind, and all the while Brody's worry shifted between his patients and Katharine.

⟶✖✖⟶

Five hours later, dusty and bearing scrapes from helping pull men from the rubble, Brody stabled his horse with Otis and entered the clinic through the back entrance. Ethan planned to stop at the clinic before he and Ben returned to the ranch. Too filthy to look in on his patients, he stepped back outside and beat as much of the dust from his clothes as possible. When he reentered and closed the door, he poured fresh water from a pitcher into a large bowl and washed the dirt and blood from his face and hands. When he reached for a clean towel, the water held evidence of his grueling afternoon.

He changed into a clean shirt and decided a bath would have to wait until he assured himself all had gone well for Katharine. His gaze moved to the ceiling, where the faint sound of a woman's voice drifted down.

The front door of the clinic opened and closed. "Brody?"

He walked to the entrance where Ethan stood at the base of the steps. "Is Ben with you?"

Ethan shook his head. "He's helping Tom deal with the two miners we brought back down. They got a little banged up but nothing serious. I want to check in on Loren and Joanna."

"I was just going up."

Loren walked in from the kitchen carrying a tray with tea and bread. "I hope you don't mind, Doc. I figure Joanna might be up soon and hungry."

"She will, and she should eat, but perhaps . . . Where is Miss Kiely?"

Loren looked from one man to the other. "Thought she was with you."

Brody passed the two men and rushed up the stairs, skipping a few at a time. When he reached the landing, he recognized Joanna's voice. Hearing Loren and Ethan on the steps behind him, he walked down the hallway to the far room and pushed opened the door.

"Kate!"

He was by her side in two strides. She sat limp against the bed, with her head and an arm resting on the edge to prevent her from sliding down. Broken glass crunched under his boots. Ignoring all else, he lifted Katharine into his arms and laid her gingerly on the bed. When he adjusted her position, a bright red stain remained on the pillow covering.

With great care, Brody pressed around the back of her head until he found the wound.

"Good God, Brody. What happened?" Ethan asked, as he walked to the foot of the bed.

He didn't answer right away. Brody found water, lukewarm, in a bowl on the dresser, and a single, clean cloth, which he wet. He staunched the trickling flow of blood with the damp cloth and kept two fingers at her pulse to assure himself her heart still beat.

"What can I do, Brody?"

He looked down at the floor and side of the bed, noticing now more blood, but not enough to cause him too much concern. Most of it had matted in her hair. "She might have a concussion, but I won't know how long she's been like this until she wakes up. My other patient's missing."

"Was she well enough to leave on her own?"

Brody shook his head as he continued to watch Katharine's face for signs of awakening. "No. She couldn't have gone far. I doubt she could have made it down the stairs without causing herself more injury."

Ethan clamped a hand on Brody's shoulder. "Look after her. I'll check in on Loren and Joanna. I'm surprised neither of them heard anything."

"Joanna wouldn't have. I gave her some herbs to help her sleep." Brody situated the cloth in a way so it remained pressed to the wound when he moved his hand away. "I need to check on Joanna. If I hadn't—"

"Don't," Ethan started. "You can't be everywhere at one time, Brody."

"I should have been here." With a last touch against her throat, he left the room and walked a few doors down to where Joanna was attempting to sit up in bed.

Loren pleaded with his wife and sought an ally in the doctor. "Will you tell her she can't be doing this, Doc?"

Brody kept his personal anguish hidden and raised a brow at his obstinate patient. "When Miss Kiely expressed worry about your recovery, I assured her you would be more annoyed at the inconvenience. Glad to see I was right."

Joanna settled her head back on the pillows. "I heard commotion."

Brody stepped forward to check Joanna's heart rate. He counted each pulse beat he felt on her wrist. "I hoped you would have slept longer. Your body will need a lot of rest the next few days."

"I'm not so old I don't know something's happened, Doc." Joanna admonished him with both words and a look that said she wouldn't be ignored. "How many times have I helped look after folks around here? A lot, I tell you."

Satisfied that she wasn't working herself into a fit, Brody released her wrist and cast a wry glance at Loren. "Is she always like this when ill?"

Joanna's aged, yet firm hand, latched onto Brody's arm. "What's happened?"

He sobered. "Miss Kiely has been

injured and the other patient is missing."

"You go look after our Katharine. I'm fit as a fiddle in here." She released his arm and waved him away. "Who's going to find the young lady. She was in no condition—"

"I am." Ethan stood in the doorway. "We'll find her." He barely made a sound with his boots as he walked down the hall.

Brody caught up with Ethan before he closed the front door. "Whoever took her could be the same person who hurt her. If she's still alive, she won't have long, Ethan."

Ethan lifted himself smoothly into the saddle and spoke a few quiet words to his horse. "Tom's been with us up at the mine, so he won't have heard about this. I'll let him know and pull enough men together to search. If anyone can track them, it's Colton. He left a little earlier than we did."

Brody wanted to argue that Colton had already spent enough time tracking the man who had shot Joanna. He had a job at the ranch and a new wife . . . every argument faded before he could voice them. "Thanks, Ethan."

Ethan nodded once before he and horse moved as one and disappeared around the corner. Brody closed the front door and returned upstairs to Katharine's side. Her listless body showed no signs of life except for the rise and fall of her chest with each breath. "You didn't come here for this," he whispered. Brody pushed aside the emotions he was not ready to identify and looked upon her as a doctor would a patient. "Come back, Kate."

14

DEEP BENEATH SKIN, flesh, and bone, the onslaught of her own thoughts pulsed against the edges of her brain. She moved her head side to side and pushed back against the soft surface. The throbbing continued, and when she could stand it no more, her mind found consciousness.

"Stop it! Please, make it stop." Her strangled whisper resounded as a shout echoed off her skull.

"It's all right, Kate."

"No, it's not." She opened her eyes and immediately shut them again. The pain worsened when light entered. "Please turn down the lamp."

When she tested her sight again, the room slowly came into focus. The light, dim now, offered little illumination. Katharine allowed herself a minute to gain her bearings. She already knew Brody was with her. She had difficulty remembering a time now when he wasn't. "How long have I been asleep?"

"I don't know exactly. It was nearly five hours before I returned from the mine." He reached beneath her shoulders and urged her to drink from the cup against her lips. "Just a sip or two. I need to make sure you can keep it down."

She gave the task of keeping her upright over to Brody and drank what he allowed. The cool liquid stung her parched throat and offered some relief once it passed. "Did you find her?"

"Not yet."

"I want to sit up."

Brody turned back the bedding and slid one arm beneath her legs. The other he used to brace her upper body as he lifted and moved her toward the headboard. Once comfortable, he covered her again with the sheet and quilt. "Tell me right away if you begin to feel a lightness in your head."

Katharine flattened the heel of a hand against her temple. "There is a terrible vibration somewhere." She moved her fingers over the crown of her head. "My hair is damp."

"I had to wash it to clean away the blood and tend to your injury."

She pictured him performing the intimate act and immediately shifted her thoughts in a new direction.

"The pain will ease soon." He held another cup out for her to take. "The tea has ginger and willow. It should help with the headache and prevent nausea from the head wound."

She inhaled the woodsy fragrance. "How much should I drink?"

"All of it, but drink slowly and let each swallow settle before drinking more."

Katharine drank as instructed while she studied the bedroom. It was not one of the recovery rooms upstairs. A bureau filled one corner and an armoire another. A desk and chair faced the window that looked out to a row of trees. The bed she sat in filled half of the tidy and lived-in room. Of course, a man of his height would need a generous bed.

She almost pulled her hand away when Brody took her wrist to check her pulse. As they sat in the silence, she wondered what his heartbeat would sound like. "You're talking and taking fluids. I don't think you've suffered a concussion, but I have no way of knowing for certain. Do you remember what happened?"

She held the warm cup of tea in the palms of both hands and breathed in the wafting aroma. It calmed her long enough so she could organize her mind. "I think her name is Mary. She said it when I walked into the room and right before she shouted at me to go away."

"Mary is what we'll call her for now. She shouted at you?"

Katharine nodded. "I think she was trying to warn me. It happened so fast, and I didn't see him, or I assume it was a man. He made no noise and before I came upstairs, she gave no warning that someone else was here. We need to find her, Finn."

"All we can do to find her is being done. Ethan was with me when I found you." He said it in a way that she believed meant

Ethan was handling everything.

"Oh, dear." She sat forward. "Were Joanna and Loren harmed?"

"Careful. You'll make the headache worse if you move too quickly."

An unfortunate truth Katharine became aware of when the pressure in her skull increased. She leaned back. "They are well?"

"As though nothing happened. From what they told me, both Loren and Joanna slept through it."

"They were resting when I brought the tea tray upstairs." She noticed for the first time a lack of sunlight seeping around the thick curtains hanging from the windows. "What time is it?"

"Almost half-past eight in the evening." Brody frowned as he watched her. "You slept far too long. I worried you wouldn't wake up."

"Other than the pounding in my head, I do not think my body has suffered too much. I should have known how fearful Mary was when I first glimpsed her. I saw her lean against the small table next to the bed, and it looked as though she was struggling to stand. It happened too fast, Finn, and I couldn't stop him."

"It wasn't you, Kate. I should have been here."

She drew on a small store of strength and pushed aside the bedding. This time she moved her legs to hang off the edge. Her wrinkled skirt offered some resistance, but she breathed deeply without constraint. The doctor had removed her corset. She might have blushed were it not for the quick knowledge that she had been a patient, and Brody did what any good doctor would have done. As far as she could tell, the rest of her clothes, including her chemise, had been put back to rights.

"Where do you think you're going?"

"As you said, I have slept too long, and you cannot stay by my side when others may need your help." Katharine used his nearness to brace herself against him as she stood and found her balance. "Ooh."

"I told you not to move too quickly."

She took in a few sharp breaths. "I forgot. I will need more of whatever tea you gave me before."

"You need to lie back down." He spoke with authority, yet made no move to help her back in bed. "And since you're as stubborn as you ever were, I won't bother to say it again. You can sit in the kitchen or . . ." he pressed a finger to her lips, ". . . there's a cushioned chair in my office where you can rest. Bessie and Stewart have been by three times since they learned you were hurt. I had to promise them on my own life that you were all right."

The events of the past few days elevated to the top of Katharine's thoughts all at once as she labored against the onslaught. "Finn."

"I've got you." Brody lifted her into his arms and carried her downstairs and into his office. He lowered her into his soft chair with a directive. "Unless you want to be off your feet longer, you'll give yourself time to rest and heal. Head wounds are dangerous, and you were alone for too long." Brody exhaled a sharp breath before he continued. "If you won't do it for yourself, do it for your father. Do you have any idea what it would do to him if something happened to you?"

Katharine stared at Brody, uncertain of his mood. "You are right to be upset. I promise to try not to do anything foolish. I intend on keeping my plans to have luncheon with Brenna at the ranch tomorrow."

"A wagon ride will exacerbate your head injury."

"I am going, Finn."

"You drive a saint mad, Kate, always did." He smiled in a way that told her he did not consider it an undesirable trait. "You and Joanna are terrible patients." Brody laid a wool blanket over her legs and headed for the door. "I'll be sending a wire to your father. Calm down, it's just a hello so he won't be worrying about you."

"Do you have pen and paper I may use to write him a letter?"

Brody looked at her oddly but retrieved a few sheets of plain paper and one of Waterman's newer fountain pens, the same kind her father favored. She smiled thinking of a rural doctor bothering with such fineries.

"You'll arrive home long before a letter does."

Katharine had not told him her plans, for she still did not know them herself, and she did not wish to speculate on them now. She needed a clear mind and the pounding at her temples did not allow for unhampered thinking. "It will help me pass the time. And please send Bessie and Stewart in. I suspect they may be waiting somewhere close by."

"I know they are." He stopped at the threshold and returned to open a window. "There's a chill, but the fresh air will do you good." Brody surprised her next by moving a small, taller table from the corner and setting it next to the chair. He left the door to his office ajar, and Katharine heard him walk down the short hallway.

She stared at the paper and for the first time in her life she had no idea what to say to her father.

15

KATHARINE DECIDED SHE had missed out as an only child. All around her, colorful personalities and cheerful voices vied for attention. Laughter and light filled the dining room as a cool and welcoming breeze blew in through the open windows, bringing with it the scents of ranch life and mountain air.

She studied each adult at the table and noted more than once that their smiles and good cheer were more for the benefit of the children than each other. On the slow ride to the ranch the day after her injury, Brody explained neither the young woman nor the man suspected of shooting

Joanna and possibly kidnapping the woman had been found. His voice had held such conviction that they would be, and Katharine prayed he was not wrong.

Absent from the table were Colton Dawson and Ramsey Cameron. Ethan and Gabriel each left briefly, and once they returned to the table, did not mention their absence.

Katharine listened to Catherine Rose, or Catie as she preferred, the girl adopted into the Gallagher family, speak of going to college in two years. Isabelle, Gabriel's wife, glowed as a woman carrying a child does. She shared her own story of arriving in Briarwood to be the schoolteacher, and how her young brother, Andrew, was becoming a fine horseman. On and on, the delightful tales of adventure continued, and with each one, Katharine's heart and mind churned with unrealized prospects.

Brody sat beside her and chuckled occasionally. She suspected he had heard some of the stories before.

"Would you like to see more of the ranch?"

She checked herself and sought whoever asked the question, and her gaze landed on Ethan. "I'm not dressed for riding."

Brenna waved away the concern. "We can get you outfitted for a ride if you'd like to go, if you're feeling well enough now after what happened."

"Quite well." Katharine had given in to Brody's request that she rest for a few more days, especially after Brenna had shown up at the clinic to explain luncheon would need to be moved. She changed the time to Sunday after services. Brody had not even tried to look contrite for his part in Brenna's convenient new plan. "The doctor has declared me fit. However, it has been five years since I last rode a horse."

Ethan said, "There's a tame mare that would suit you."

She looked to Brody. "If anyone else needs your services—"

"We can spare a little time. Joanna is resting at home, and you said yourself Bessie is happier having someone to look after. Folks know where I am, and we won't be too long." Brody glanced at Ethan who nodded in confirmation. "How are you feeling?"

"You have already said I am well enough, and my head hasn't hurt once in the past two days. I would like to go." Katharine allowed Brenna to guide her from the dining room and up the stairs.

Fifteen minutes later, she had traded her out-of-place dress of the latest fashion with a serviceable white shirt tucked into a comfortable riding skirt. A fitted vest and long canvas duster coat completed the ensemble. Gone was the corset she never liked and the fitted skirt her dressmaker had designed without a bustle.

Freedom to move and breathe elevated her excitement at the pending ride.

"Whatever is wrong?"

She faced Brenna. "Nothing. I like how the clothes feel."

"They are practical, but I don't speak of the clothes. Your smile vanished."

Katharine picked up the pair of leather gloves Brenna had left out. "Brody's patient is missing and possibly worse. Joanna will heal, but she could have died, and the man who injured her is still free."

"And you think this means you should not smile?"

"It sounds foolish, I know, but what right do I have to—"

"Whit's fur ye'll no go by ye." Brenna

grasped Katharine's hands in a fist. "What's meant to happen will happen. Life does not pause when the world around us is in chaos, a lesson I learned after my mother died and again after my father's passing. Every moment of joy we can capture is in our right, be it one minute or one day. I believe in Tom, Colton, Ramsey, and all the others who are taking shifts to search for the young woman. Mary is her name, yes?"

Katharine nodded. "I think so."

"Ethan and Gabriel were out half the night. Ramsey and Ben left early this morning. If she is out there, they will find her. Until then, we feed the men, care for the children, and send food to the widows at the family mining camp. We do what we can for as long as we can, and in between, we hold on to every precious piece of good we are able."

"There are two camps?"

"One for the bachelors closer to the mines and another one for the married men. The houses are a little larger and sit half a mile farther away. It's safer for the children." Brenna seemed genuinely surprised. "You didn't know?"

"No, that information was not included. We were told only bachelors worked the mines. Are there many families?"

"Only four right now, and two widows with young children. If they don't remarry in the first few months, they'll either move to town or leave the territory. Some have started over here, but most of the widows leave."

She could not fathom losing a husband and then having to make such a life-altering decision soon after. Katharine's more immediate concern was learning more about the camp which would require a visit.

Brenna squeezed her hands and walked from the room, saying over her shoulder, "I will be only a few minutes if you want to wait downstairs."

Katharine thought of the letter she wrote to her father yesterday, still in her reticule and of Brenna's words: *Every moment of joy we can capture, is in our right, be it one minute or one day.*

A few minutes later, she walked downstairs, and Brody waited for her near the front door. His grin started small and widened as she approached. "Ye're a bonny lass, Katharine Kiely. The clothes suit you."

She thought again of Brenna's words and returned his grin with one of her own. "Do you mean to say my own clothes do not?" His cheeks took on a slight red hue, and she rebuked herself for the bold words.

"You know well enough . . . There are no words I can say now to not sound like a fool."

He held the door open for her and followed her onto the front porch. A few minutes later, Brenna joined them. It surprised Katharine to see Ethan's horse saddled and waiting near the others. Brody showed her the horse she would ride, but one look at the distance between ground and saddle, and Katharine stepped back, uncertain how to manage. Brody solved the problem when he came up beside her.

"How long has it been?"

"Five years."

"You'll remember the basics, then. Put your left hand on the horn there and grip the back of the saddle with your right hand. Good. Now, put your left foot in the stirrup."

Katharine tried and failed. "This is embarrassing."

"Let's try again." This time Brody's large hands held onto her waist and lifted as she pulled up. With little effort she found herself seated in a comfortably worn saddle. "Has your headache returned? Sometimes being up higher from the ground can cause one to be lightheaded if they've suffered a head injury."

"Quit your worrying. I feel quite good. A little stiff, perhaps, and anxious. I am not certain why."

Brody squeezed her hand without offering a suggestion as to her current predicament. He mounted a tall, red gelding and motioned her ahead of him to ride alongside Brenna between him and Ethan. Katharine did not know why exactly, but she somehow felt this was one moment that would define the rest of her life.

16

MIST SHROUDED THE valley and grazed Katharine's skin. Water tumbled and gurgled over rocks nearby, though the source remained hidden beyond a smattering of trees, lush in green against the overwhelming strength of the mountain at which base she now sat.

She closed her eyes and concentrated on the subtle instruments of nature's music. While finishing a project in Colorado, her father took her to The Tabor Opera House in Denver during its first week in September 1881. The phenomenal operatic talent of Emma Abbot had filled the hall that night. It was a rare experience for Katharine, and one she fondly remembered. Yet, no sounds on earth soothed and inspired her soul as those released from the tree and bird or river and wind.

The land hummed and her vibrations rose from the soil to blend with the wind as it caressed the trees, creating a symphonic sound with which no string quartet could compete.

"Katharine?"

Her eyes fluttered open in protest, for the intrusion, though kindly met, broke the song before it reached its crescendo. She looked at Brenna who sat atop a pretty, speckled mare and offered her new friend a smile.

"You drifted away."

Yes, Katharine thought, she had, and what a beautiful, albeit brief, ramble with nature it had been. "I have stood among great landscapes of America's vast West. Her territories abound with beautiful mountains so tall one can never imagine climbing them, and rivers wide enough to carry more water than anyone could ever need, and yet . . ."

Brenna moved her mare closer. "And yet?"

"What is so different about this place?"

"Oh, my dear." Brenna smoothed a hand over Katharine's arm. "You're crying."

Katharine denied it until the first tear dampened her lashes and slid over her cheek. "I don't know why. There is no reason to, none." She wiped a gloved hand over her skin and sure enough, a damp spot now discolored the soft, beige leather.

"Come with me. I would like to show you something." Ethan and Brody sat on their horses a short distance away to give them privacy. Brenna called out over her shoulder to tell them they would not be gone long.

Brenna led her on a path through the trees and a narrow section of the creek Katharine heard earlier. Her guide remained quiet as the horses carried them a quarter mile where she finally stopped.

Brenna beckoned her to dismount. "Do not worry, there is a rock just over there when it is time to get back up."

Grateful for a few minutes to move her legs, Katharine carefully swung a leg over and did not release her grip on the saddle until her feet touched the ground. The slight jarring gave her head a brief shot of pain before it quickly subsided. "I am indebted to Eliza for loan of the riding skirt."

"She has a wardrobe filled with them for the times she cannot reasonably wear the trousers she has special made for ranch work."

"Does Briarwood have a seamstress?" Katharine asked, as she followed Brenna's lead and loosely wrapped the horse's reins around a low-hanging tree branch.

"We did for a long time, but she married and they moved to Cheyenne last spring." Brenna motioned Katharine to join her.

The view below did not require an introduction or explanation. Down the gentle sweep of rock, where a narrow trail cut into the mountain, a wide valley spread unexpectedly before them. The breath Katharine had not realized she was holding escaped slowly. She felt first her lips relax, then her cheeks, eyes, and soon her entire body, which filled with an awesome sense of relief and calm.

No rail or road cut through the valley, leaving it for the wild creatures who walked, ran, and slept on the land long before any of the current tenants. A small herd of horses grazed on the early autumn grass kept green by recent rains.

"Do those belong to the ranch?"

"No, there are a few wild herds in the territory, and these live in this valley part of the year. We don't see them during the winter. Colton once told me they spend most of the winter months in another valley some miles from here, where they are more protected and there is a stream that flows all year, much like ours."

Katharine watched the horses meander and pick at what they must have deemed the sweetest grasses and shrubs. "Was it difficult for you when you decided to make Montana your home?" She looked at Brenna. "Everything and everyone you knew was so far away. Do you miss it?"

Brenna's soft smile brightened her face

with an unmistakable look of love. "Every day, but my family here keeps the sadness from creeping into my heart."

"Will you return?"

"Aye." She smiled brighter. "Ethan and I planned to take the children a few times to visit Scotland. Life has delayed us so far, though we have promised each other, and the children, to visit next year. Rebecca will be old enough to withstand with the journey by then. Colton and Ainslee, his new bride and my cousin, will leave soon. I wish you could have met her today. She and Colton live in a cabin near Ramsey and Eliza's house. She came for a visit recently, and she wants Colton to meet her family."

"Family," Katharine murmured. She thought of her father and her quiet, predictable, though comfortable, life in Astoria. "Thank you for sharing this special place with me. Does it have a name?"

"Colton calls it by a native name I cannot pronounce, but Ethan told me it translates roughly to 'Valley Where the Light Shines Longest.' The family, if they call it anything, refer to it as 'Valley of Dreams,' as do those in town."

"Others come here?"

Brenna smiled at Katharine. "By law and deed the Gallagher family owns this land, but it doesn't belong to them. So long as people respect it, they know they are welcome to visit this spot."

Katharine studied the valley again as she thought Brenna might see it. She noticed the snow on the highest of the peaks glittered when clouds moved away to allow the sun access. One of the hawks Brody spoke of flew low and was soon joined by another. Their dance conveyed more of their bond than the formal ones she witnessed between man and woman.

"Is there always snow up there this early in autumn?"

"It is the middle of September." Brenna released a light laugh. "I have seen snow fall three feet this time of year. Another year, the snow did not come until well into October."

Katharine wondered now about the journey home. "The leaves have barely turned."

"Gabriel and Ethan said just yesterday how they expect an early winter. The colors will come sooner than you might expect."

Katharine imagined the landscape in a cascade of color and doubted her imagination did the full height of autumn justice. She returned to her tethered horse, walked the animal to the rock

Brenna pointed out earlier, and climbed into the saddle. She would be sore all over tomorrow. "Did Ethan know you would show me this valley when Gabriel asked if I could ride?"

Brenna walked her horse a few feet away. "Yes."

"They wanted me to see it. Why?"

"Can you not guess?"

Katharine stopped her mare. "Brenna, my father won't do business with the mine. I give you my word."

"Ethan knows that." Brenna started moving again and stayed close as they followed the wide trail back through the trees. "The entire family has fought for a long time to protect this land, and Ethan more than the others. He sees it as a stewardship and a calling. Ethan wanted you to see this place for the same reason Colton brought Ainslee here before they wed and why Ethan showed me. One cannot stand in such a place and not feel the earth's heart beating all around them."

Katharine contemplated Brenna's words and remained silent as they came out on the other side of the trees. Ethan and Brody had followed them so they would be close enough if trouble arose. She believed Ethan would always be close when his wife needed him, and with that thought, her eyes shifted and settled on Brody.

They reached the lower pasture thirty minutes later, with the houses and outbuildings in sight. Katharine did not know which of them heard the shouts first, but they all saw the rider coming toward them at a speed too fast for it to be safe. With amazing skill, the rider, a man she had not yet met, brought his horse to a dancing stop.

"Doc, there's trouble in town." The rider

wiped sweat from his face. "Ethan, I'm to tell you Ramsey and Colton have returned. They've found something."

Brody reached for her hand. "How's your head? The drive back will be—"

"No. Go, now, without me. I will get back to town." When he hesitated, she added. "Go, Finn. I will be fine."

Ethan's next words indicated he heard their conversation. "Take the horse, Brody. We'll get him later, and I'll see Katharine safely to town."

Brody gave her one last, long look before he coaxed the horse into a gallop. He stopped long enough to grab his medical bag from under the front seat of the wagon they had driven to the ranch, and seconds later, man and horse raced toward Briarwood. It was a familiar sight, and she watched with a heady mix of both pride and sadness.

17

BRODY ENTERED TOWN on the frenzy of concern Florence Lloyd had carried with him to Hawk's Peak. The young man had stayed behind long enough to cool his horse down and get it water, but Brody could not wait. Without details, he did not know what to expect when he rode into Briarwood.

The shouts and crowd of people standing in front of his clinic were enough to slow his pulse. Crisis fueled him, calmed him, and always triggered in him all the knowledge and composure required to get him through an emergency.

What had happened in the few hours

since his departure? Brody slowed his horse and dismounted. All at once, the explanations and concerns encroached on his space, and he held a hand up high to get everyone's attention.

"One at a time, please." He addressed Flora Carver, who stood on the porch. There was no reason for the schoolteacher to be here unless something happened to one of her students. "Flora?"

"The Rowland family have four children. Doc, three of them are sick."

Brody brushed past a few of the townsfolk trying to figure out why they were there. Turning to Flora, he asked, "How are the Rowlands?"

"They arrived last night and are camped on the outskirts of town."

"The parents?"

Flora clutched the edge of her apron, the front stained with evidence of cooking.

"All right, I think. I was helping Tilly with the baking for Sunday when they came looking for help."

"What's going on, Doc?"

"Can't be letting no sick people spread something, Doc!"

"Are we safe?"

The questions came from all directions, and once again, Brody held up a hand. "My only concern right now are the sick children inside. Go home, all of you." Brody shook his head when Flora followed. "Was anyone else in contact with the family?"

"I don't think so, but I can't be sure."

"Good. Go home, Flora, and stay there until I come to you. Please don't stop and talk to anyone."

Flora clutched her neck. "You think—"

"I think nothing yet. It's merely a precaution. Fix yourself a cup of the flower tea you like, and I'll be along soon."

Flora nodded and remained on the porch when he closed the door firmly behind him. If the children were contagious, he couldn't risk the illness spreading to others. He heard the inaudible murmurs in his surgery before he saw the family . . . four children. The daughter appeared unaffected, but the three boys showed troubling color, and one of them had rapid breathing. He went to this child first, who also appeared to be the youngest, and lifted him onto the examination table.

He spoke to the parents while he washed his hands and wiped them with alcohol. "I'm Doctor Brody. I've just been told your children are feeling poorly."

The father stepped forward while the mother held the only daughter close. "I'm Denny Rowland and this here is my wife,

Ada. That young 'un there is Otto."

Brody momentarily blocked out the father's voice while he listened to the boy's lungs. "What other symptoms have the children shown?"

Ada Rowland said with an edge of panic in her voice, "Fever and chills. They sleep a lot and don't want to eat."

Brody knuckled the chin of young Otto, a boy he guessed to be five. "Does it hurt when you swallow? When you put food down your throat?"

The boy shook his head, his eyes pinched.

"Does your head hurt?"

The boy nodded this time.

Brody fetched a silver tongue depressor from his clean instrument supply. "Is it all right if I look at your throat?" Brody opened his mouth wide to show the boy. Uncertain, Otto slowly mimicked Brody.

He inserted the depressor and raised Otto's chin a little more and found only an inflamed throat, likely from too much coughing. "Where did you travel here from, Mr. Rowland?"

"Outside Boise City."

"Idaho. In which direction did you travel?" Brody faced the man. "My questions sound odd, but they will help with the diagnosis."

Denny scratched his chin. "East. Camped along the Bitterroot for a spell. Got a brother outside Frenchtown."

Brody raised the sleeves of the boy's shirt and noticed the unmistakable blotches. "Is this the first time the children have experienced such symptoms?"

Denny clutched his other two son's hands. "First time. These two don't have it so bad, but Otto's been in fierce pain."

"I need to examine the other boys, and it

would be best to do it one at a time. You may stay in the room with us, Mr. Rowland. Mrs. Rowland, I'll ask you and your daughter to wait outside with the other two boys until we're ready for them." He looked the family over again. "Or perhaps the kitchen. Tilly always brings over fresh cornbread on Thursdays from her café."

"That's mighty kind of you, Doc."

Denny encouraged his wife to take their daughter and two sons into the other room. Brody returned a few minutes later after seeing them settled. "We're going to examine your son's skin carefully. I'll need you to stay close, so he knows he's safe."

With his father's help, Brody quickly found what he feared on Otto's torso and ankles. The spots lightened when applied with gentle pressure. He searched carefully along the boy's hairline for further evidence. "I can't make a definitive diagnosis because a test does not yet exist to confirm, and I have only seen one case before, but based on the symptoms, and what you've told me, I believe your son has contracted a bacterium from the bite of a tick. I have heard about outbreaks along the Bitterroot River."

"All three boys?"

Brody washed his hands and wiped them again with alcohol. "It is possible, but I will need to examine them to be certain."

Denny helped Otto back on with his shoes. "Is he going to be okay?"

Brody dried his hands and cast a glance at the boy. "I want to speak with you and your wife alone after I see to the other children."

A half hour later, Brody found similar signs, though less severe, on the other two boys. The girl did not exhibit any symptoms and was without a rash. He waited for the parents to settle their children at the long table and follow him back into the examination room. "There is no cure for what we call black measles. It isn't like measles you've probably heard of before. This is a tick fever, and I need to caution you both—please, sit down Mrs. Rowland." He helped lower her to a bench beneath the window before continuing.

She muffled a soft sob. "Is my boy going to be okay?"

"This is a serious illness, and I will not lie to you about the risks. It can be fatal—"

Mrs. Rowland grasped her husband's arm and leaned into him.

"It isn't contagious, but I would like you to stay here in the rooms upstairs, so I can monitor all three of your sons. The older two have mild symptoms. The severity of Otto's does concern me."

"Will he die?" Denny asked, as his wife cried into his worn jacket.

"I don't know, Mr. Rowland, but know I will do everything I can."

The pain-filled voice of the man asking if his son would live or die kept Katharine just outside of sight. She covered her mouth and closed her eyes against the forming tears. Her breath shuddered once before she composed herself and followed the soft sounds of children talking.

All at once, the four tired faces looked at her. "I'm Katharine, a friend of Doctor Brody's."

The boy who appeared to be the oldest said, "He's talking with Ma and Pa."

"They won't be much longer." Katharine walked across the room and helped herself to a glass of water from a pitcher someone recently had filled. The tepid liquid soothed her parched throat and gave her a few seconds to study each of the children. She saw immediately the telltale signs of fever in all three boys, but it was the youngest, a small child with unruly light brown hair and big brown eyes, who appeared frighteningly frail.

"That's a fancy dress."

Katharine gave her attention to the girl who made the statement. She smoothed a hand over the front of her bodice. "I suppose it is." She preferred the riding clothes she had borrowed from Eliza. "Do you like it?" she asked, hoping to engage the children and draw their focus from the conversation down the hall. They could not hear the words spoken, but the air vibrated with tense energy.

The parents preceded Brody into the

room, and the mother immediately went to the smallest boy. Katharine caught the momentary surprise in Brody's expression at her presence, but he quickly collected himself and introduced her to Denny and Ada Rowland. They spared her a look only long enough to be polite and gave all their attention to the children.

"Come along, Otto." Denny Rowland lifted the youngest, and most sickly looking, child into his arms. "We're going to stay in this nice place for a little while. How d'you like that?"

"With a bed?" the boy whispered.

His father pressed a kiss to his brow. "With a bed. The doctor here tells me this place has running water that turns on and off. How 'bout that?"

Brody led them all to the stairs. "I will be up soon after I gather a few things to help with the fever. There are no other patients in the rooms upstairs, and we have changed the bedding."

The parents ushered the young ones up the stairs. Katharine heard soft sounds of excitement when they entered the rooms and she felt shame for her finery. "I should have waited outside."

"You're a welcome sight." Brody started for the surgery room again. "Will you join me?"

Katharine followed and immediately said, "What can I do to help?"

Brody asked a question of his own. "Where is Ethan?"

"He went to the sheriff's office to meet with Ramsey, Colton, and . . ."

"Ben."

"Yes. The sheriff was outside the saloon when we rode in. He took your wagon to the livery."

Brody nodded began taking small jars of

herbs down from a tall black shelf filled with a variety of amber bottles, clear glass jars, and metal tins, and arranged them on a large, wooden tray. "Ethan will come by when he can to tell us what he's learned," Brody said with confidence as he measured some herbs into individual cups. "You can fetch the kettle on the stove. The water should still be hot enough to make this tea."

Katharine retrieved the heavy kettle and placed it within Brody's reach. "What kind of tea?"

"Yarrow to help reduce their fevers. Once they've finished these, they'll get a syrup made of elderberries, honey, and cinnamon."

"Those aren't medicines, Finn."

He glanced up at her. "There is no medicine for what they have. All I can do is treat the fever, try to keep them comfortable, and hope they survive. It's tick fever and often fatal in young children."

Katharine removed her hat and jacket and slipped into one of the familiar aprons. "What can I do?"

"This isn't for you, Kate. You should be at home by the sea, spending—"

"Finn, please."

Brody tucked a stray strand of hair behind her ear, which both warmed and surprised her. "I've grown used to your company and your help, after such a short time. Add half a teaspoon of sugar into each cup. It will help cut the bitterness."

For the next several hours, Katharine learned what it was to be a nurse. She fetched water and clean linens, went down to Tilly's, ordering enough food for the family of six, with the request for three meals a day, until Brody said otherwise.

She accepted the chore to inform Flora, the schoolteacher, that the illness was not contagious, and no one was in danger. Katharine left the woman's house with a promise that Flora would share the news around town.

She made tea for the children and coffee for the parents and read to the Rowland girl, Grace, when her mother's emotional exhaustion prevented her from doing so.

"Is Otto going to be all right?"

Katharine smoothed back a tangled curl and peered down at Grace. "My father once told me that God put all the people with the biggest hearts and gentlest souls through the most hardships, for they are the only ones strong enough."

"I don't understand."

She looked up and saw Brody in the doorway. Katharine kept her voice light even as the need to cry overwhelmed her.

"You will know one day. Now, let's get you ready for bed. Doc Brody has a nice big bathing tub in a room just down the hall. You turn on a knob and out comes the water."

Otherwise occupied now, Grace nodded with enthusiasm and scooted off the bed. "Wait till I tell Otto. Do you think he'll get a bath, too?"

18

THE BENCH ON the front porch of the clinic creaked a little as Katharine rested against the back of the sturdy piece of furniture, even though it looked older than the building. In the distance, above the meadow, stars splashed across the sky as the town settled in for the evening. She heard enough voices to know the town's only two open establishments at this time of night—Tilly's Café and the saloon—were busy.

The door next to her opened softly. Brody left it ajar and took the place beside her on the bench.

"What are Otto's chances?"

"Not good."

Katharine nodded and continued to stare up at the stars. "They seem to be good people, who sought to start a new life. It is sad, really, how easily hopes and dreams can be quashed in a single moment."

"They'll make it through this."

"How can they possibly? I remember the immediate days after I lost my mother. I can only imagine the pain is far worse when it is someone's child. Have you seen this before, this what did you call it? Black measles?"

"Once in an adult, but it was a young and healthy man. Children, however, are at greater risk." Brody recalled something one of his professors had said to him at medical school and hoped it would bring her comfort now. "Life is too precious not to acknowledge the difficulty when someone suffers, but it is also too precious to give up hope after someone dies." Brody draped an arm over her shoulders and drew her close. "I'm sorry, Kate, that I wasn't there when your mother passed."

She allowed herself to seek comfort in his embrace and relaxed her body. "Father took us away so quickly after it happened. He didn't want to remain where everything reminded him of her."

"Have you been happy?"

Katharine leaned away from him. "I remember being a happy child. These last ten years have kept me too busy to think much on it. Stewart posted my letter yesterday, and my father will no doubt expect me home soon."

Brody pulled back his arm and sat straighter. "Will you continue to work with him?"

"I have not decided what I will do beyond tomorrow."

"What happens tomorrow?"

"What transpired with the mine has bothered me. Mr. Jameston's delay in meeting with me, and his reaction later when I told him there would be no help from Kiely Limited, are both troubling. I have asked—" Katharine stood, and Brody quickly joined her. "Bessie and Stewart are coming."

Bessie spoke first when the duo approached. "Mrs. Baker is well. She said she's never been so spoiled as this. She's been resting since moving to her own bed this morning, just as you instructed, Doctor." The maid smiled and gained an equal reaction from the others.

Brody said, "I appreciate your care of her. Please let her know I will be by tomorrow."

Bessie bent her head forward slightly in a respectful nod. Katharine watched with interest and realized the other woman's inherent etiquette remained intact no matter how casual the circumstances. She had never paid attention before now.

"Stewart, I need to speak with you in a moment, but to both of you, I wish to say it is time to return home."

An array of emotions crossed over everyone's faces. On Brody she saw a stiff jaw as he looked away. Bessie's face showed extreme relief and a touch of joy, and Stewart seemed like a man freed from the gallows.

Stewart asked, "When will we be leaving, Miss Kiely?"

"You, Bessie, and the brothers will leave the day after tomorrow. There is enough time to purchase all the necessary provisions. I am certain there will be someone in town willing to hire on until you reach Butte where you can board the train. We will wire ahead to make sure there is a cargo hold available for all the equipment."

Katharine shook her head when Stewart and Bessie spoke at once. "This is how it will be. I will not ask you to remain here when there is no reason, and I am not ready to leave."

"Your father won't be liking it, Miss Kiely."

"My father will understand, Stewart." Katharine reminded herself that while she valued her father's opinion, she did not require it. "I will wire him again to explain and you can deliver another letter."

"How will you get home?" Bessie asked. "You can't think to stay here alone, without a chaperone."

"Bessie, you have longed to return home from the moment we stepped off the train."

"I won't leave you, Miss."

Katharine glanced from one loyal servant to the next. "You really won't go?"

Each one shook their heads, and Stewart added, "We can send the brothers on to the project in Utah. They could use the extra help to finish up."

"Very well, please make the arrangements for them. Bessie, you may retire for the evening if you wish." Bessie hesitated briefly, bowed her head slightly once again, and walked over the dirt road back to the general store. "Stewart, were you able to find anything out of the ordinary when you walked the land?"

Stewart glanced sideways at Brody.

"It is all right. You can speak freely in front of Doctor Brody. He is a friend of my father."

Stewart stepped closer to the building and lowered his voice. "I found nothing."

Of all the results Katharine expected Stewart to share, "nothing" was not among them. "You are certain? You walked the entire area?"

"I did. Some parts twice over."

"It makes no sense." Katharine lowered herself back to the bench and would have tripped backward had Brody's hand on her lower back not guided her down.

"What is it, Kate?"

She asked Stewart again, "You found nothing at all?"

"Nothing on the land you asked me to search."

"Thank you, Stewart. That will be all. We must wire my father again in the morning."

"Yes, ma'am." Stewart excused himself and walked in the direction of the saloon. He did not drink much or often, but Katharine knew he enjoyed the atmosphere of such places.

"Kate, what was that about?"

"I asked Stewart to walk the land where Mr. Jameston wanted to run the spur line. I should have spoken to the Gallaghers first, but I had hoped . . . it makes no sense for him to have found nothing."

"Because of Jameston's odd behavior?"

Katharine stood again this time close enough to Brody's legs to prevent him from also standing right away. She did not have to peer too far down for their eyes to meet. "Who would know this area better than anyone else, especially the Gallaghers' land west of town?"

Brody did not have to think on it. "Almost anyone who's lived in town more than a few months will have some knowledge. You have to know the land to survive. Colton or Ben from the ranch are the best trackers, but the family would know if there was something on their land other than . . . what were you hoping Stewart would find?"

"When I was at Tilly's this afternoon, she mentioned seeing Ethan ride east of town with Tom and two other men."

"They were probably Colton and Ramsey. Ben's the foreman, and I've never known him to stay away from the ranch for too long." Brody eased her to the right a little so he could stand without knocking her over. "Kate, slow down a minute. What did you expect to find on the land?"

"Another reason for the spur line or at least an explanation why they want access to that parcel of land."

19

BRODY STAYED AWAKE through the night to monitor the boys for new symptoms. Otto's fever elevated shortly after midnight and the nausea began soon after. By morning, he'd lost feeling in one of his feet.

Katharine remained close all the while and divided her time between sleep and looking after the other children, while Brody ministered to the youngest. The fevers on the older boys eased up, giving Brody some hope that they would recover.

As evening crept into morning, Katharine carried a pitcher of fresh water into the room on a tray with a small stack of clean cloths. "I made some coffee, though I cannot promise it will taste good. I can bring some up next time."

Brody watched her move about the room, emptying the bowl of water out a side window where it fell into the trees below, and refilling it with fresh. She stacked the new cloths neatly within his reach and spared a moment to smooth the hair off Otto's brow. Soft, dark smudges marred the skin beneath her tired eyes, but exhaustion did not hinder her dedication.

"Kate," he whispered, careful not to wake the parents who had finally fallen asleep a few hours prior. Otto's father slept slumped in a chair and his mother slept with her head and torso on the bed and her hand holding the boy's. Brody reached for Katharine, and with a light grip on her shoulders, he ushered her from the room. "You need to sleep."

She wiped a hand over her eyes. "I can't." Her shoulders lifted and fell in a long shrug. "Every time I think about resting, thoughts flood my mind."

"About what?"

"The children, their parents, the land. They will not be quieted, and so I must keep busy." She brushed a fallen tendril off her cheek. "I keep thinking about Mary, too. If she was still nearby and alive, would they not have found her?"

"You have a good heart, Kate." He tipped her head back, and had she not been so tired and her mind filled with worry, he would give into temptation. "Go for a walk. The fresh air will do you good, so will spending a little time away from here."

Brody wiped a single tear from her cheek. "All will be well."

"Not for them." Katharine peered around him. "How long does Otto have left?"

Rather than answer the question, he pulled her close and pressed a kiss to her forehead. "You'll need one of my coats for the walk."

She eased away from his embrace. "Bessie brought over my shawl yesterday. It will suffice."

Brody walked downstairs with her because he didn't trust her to leave the building without encouragement. He waited while she removed the apron and wrapped a fine, wool shawl around her shoulders. They stepped outside together, and Brody breathed in the early morning air. He counted the days since her arrival and wondered how the twenty years apart seemed to dissolve away in such a short time.

"I will see to breakfast when I return. Tilly will have it sent over soon."

"Take your time, Kate."

She paused at the first step off the porch and stared at the empty land across from his clinic. "Would you ever consider leaving this place?"

Brody had asked himself the same question many times over the years. Opportunities arose now and then for him to venture to a city where hospital jobs awaited or he could make more money. Whenever the idea surfaced, no matter the origin, he gave it careful consideration but always dismissed leaving. "I have a few times, but were I to leave this place, it would be for Ireland." He waited for her to turn around, but she kept her back to him. "This is where I need to be right now."

Katharine stepped off the porch and walked toward the meadow. He observed her for several minutes until she stopped at the footbridge, leaned against one of the wood handrails, and together they watched muted light from the sun appear over the peaks.

"Brody," a male voice said from nearby.

He drew his attention away from Katharine to the new arrivals. Ethan walked in front and with him were Colton and Ramsey. A day's worth of dust covered all three men. Going a full night without sleep was not uncommon to any of them. "When I left the ranch there had been news, but Katharine heard you'd ridden out again." Brody wanted to prescribe baths, sleep, and a hearty meal in that order. "There's coffee on the stove."

Ethan removed his hat and raked a hand through thick hair. "We're carrying too much trail dust and need to get back to the ranch soon." Ethan must have caught the direction of Brody's quick glance for he said next, "Has she been helping in the clinic again?"

"Best nurse I've ever worked with, but it's not work she should be doing."

"Unless it's what she wants."

Brody did not want to speculate on what might be best for Katharine, at least not until she told him. He already learned that one trait she had carried with her from childhood was the ability to speak and know her own mind. "Any news on Mary?"

Ramsey said, "Colton tracked the man who shot Joanna back to the mining camp, but there was no way to tell who he might be, and no one is talking."

Brody looked to Colton. "Same man who took Mary and hit Katharine?"

"Looks like. Whoever he was, he doubled back to town. The tracks left the second time included a woman's smaller pair.

How tall is Mary?"

"A few inches over five feet."

Colton nodded. "The tracks could be hers."

"So, she was in the camp, too?"

Ethan nodded. "Looks like she was. We spent most of yesterday afternoon and into the night looking for her, but nothing came of it. A pair of horses, still harnessed, were found halfway between here and an abandoned wagon. Nothing was left behind."

Brody looked out to where he last saw Katharine. She hadn't moved. "What about Jameston?"

"He wasn't there. His assistant said he went to Bozeman for a meeting." Ramsey stepped in front of Brody to get his attention. "Why do you ask about him?"

"Katharine suspects there is more to Jameston than just wanting the spur line."

To Ethan he added, "She thinks it has something to do with your land."

Colton said, "Which explains why I saw her surveyor walking around there yesterday."

Brody quickly defended Katharine's actions. "She's already said she should have spoken with you first, Ethan."

"She can search every inch of our land if it will give her answers, but I'd like to talk with her about it. What did she hope to find?"

"I asked her the same thing." Brody heard his name come from inside. "I need to get back to my patients. Ethan, if you're going to speak with her right now . . . it's been a rough night for her."

Ethan and Brody studied each other with enough of an idea of what each other was thinking to render words unnecessary. Brody hurried inside and forced his mind to clear away thoughts of Katharine while he tended to his patients.

⁂

Katharine met the men halfway across the distance she had walked. Were it not for meeting Ethan twice before, and already trusting the man and anyone else he trusted with her life, she might not have been so confident as they approached.

The early morning light cast a reddish hue across the sky, and though it remained hidden behind the tallest mountains, it offered enough light to make visible the men's expressions. Exhaustion, curiosity, and concern—she could not decide which of these they suffered from most.

Ethan tipped his hat to her. "Katharine Kiely, this is my brother-in-law, Ramsey Cameron, and this is Colton Dawson."

"I have heard of your impressive tracking skills, Mr. Dawson."

He tipped the edge of his hat to her. "Colton, please. Doing my job, ma'am."

Chivalry, it seemed, extended to all the men at the ranch. Her good humor faded when she noticed Brody no longer stood on the porch of the clinic. "Where is Brody? Did something happen with one of the children?"

She walked past, but Ethan's words stopped her. "Please, Katharine, a few minutes of your time."

Torn about leaving Brody to carry the burden alone, she gave each man a quick once over. Instead of her first thought, she went with her second. "You have been searching all night?"

"We have."

Katharine faced Ramsey, hoping for more. "Mary?"

Ethan brushed a gloved hand lightly over her arm to draw her attention. Katharine had to tilt her head back as far as she did with Brody to look directly at Ethan.

"We have not found her yet. The other search party went looking for where she might have come from on the road but didn't find anyone else. There were signs of a camp, and whoever stayed there traveled this way, but they abandoned the wagon in the trees a mile from town. The back was empty, and the search party found the horses farther down the road."

Katharine hugged herself, wrapping the shawl tighter around her upper body. "Did you tell Brody this?"

"We did, but it's not why we came over here." Ethan pointed to the clinic. "Would you prefer to sit down? You look about done in."

She shook her head. "No, please tell me."

"Brody mentioned you suspected a connection between Jameston and my land."

"I apologize for not speaking with you sooner."

"Please, I'm not upset. It's difficult to believe there'd be anything on the land we don't know about, so what do you suspect Jameston's motives are, and what could he possibly want other than the railroad? There's nothing else there."

Katharine indicated Colton with a glance. "Brody said you can find anything. Is that true?"

"Not everything is meant to be found."

She smiled, for it was exactly the response her father would give if posed the same question. "My surveyor, Stewart, told me there was nothing out of the ordinary about your land, but I believe he is wrong."

"What makes you think so?" Ethan asked.

"Experience. If you had been there when Mr. Jameston learned my father's company would not be doing business with him, he behaved contradictory to the situation. True, a spur line means more profits for the mine, and yet, this . . . It is your land and your decision."

Ethan exchanged a look with Colton, then Ramsey. "We have to head back to the ranch right now, but I promise we haven't given up on Mary, and we will search the land again. What are we looking for?"

Katharine exhaled and felt her shoulders relax. "I expect you will know when you find it." Her father had ensured she could run the business and she never genuinely appreciated all of his careful teaching until now. "If the land office has papers and maps of the plots, then I may be able to help a little more."

"They will. It might take a little time to find it with no one running the place, but Orin from the telegraph office can help. He knows his way around the land office documents better than the rest of us. I'll let him know what you need." Ethan lifted her hand into his, startling her into looking up again to meet his eyes. "You remind me a lot of my Brenna when she first came. Fire in her eyes and more determination than was good for her. Please be careful."

"I have no intention of putting myself in harm's way."

Ethan grinned and released her hand. "That's what Brenna used to say. We'll be talking soon."

Fascinated, Katharine waited until they

rode away before turning her face back to the rising sun. Her breath shuddered on the intake as clouds formed around the mountains and darkened the rich reds and light yellows spreading, then fading, into the dim blue sky. Strands of her hair fluttered about her face and the edges of her shawl billowed out behind her as she returned to the clinic.

Early risers were already going about their tasks of readying businesses and preparing for the day ahead. None appeared surprised by the shift in the sky and air when a sudden gust gathered dust and tiny pebbles and carried them down the road. The beautiful sunrise disappeared behind darkening clouds, prompting Katharine indoors.

A few minutes later, she stood in the doorway of young Otto's room, the cold outside forgotten. The boy's mother rocked him slowly with her arms enfolding him. Her husband sat next to her and held them both. She heard Grace talking with her brothers in the room next door. Denny and Ada Rowland kept their sobs quiet as Ada hummed a soft tune.

Defeated, Brody walked into the hallway and Katharine followed. "It is too fast, Finn."

"It can happen fast. I've given him all I can to minimize the pain, but I do not think he feels much of it anymore."

"My father sheltered me from the world's sadness after my mother died. It worked for many years, and as each year passed, memories from our time in South Carolina filtered into my dreams. Echoes from the cannons, the stench of acrid smoke, and cries from women who learned the hard way that death eventually touches everyone." She cleared her throat and dried her eyes. "You have devoted your life to this work, and as a child I did not comprehend what such a commitment meant. I have seen the way you smile, and how easy it is for you to laugh. How do you do it when this . . ." She waved a hand toward the room.

"The same way you found laughter after you lost your mother. Our hearts are not meant to break, Katharine. They beat life into every breath and remind us we exist for a purpose, and so long as we have life in us, all the tragedies and wonderment in this world will find us. But we still go on living."

The last time Katharine saw tears in a man's eyes was twenty years ago when her father stood over his wife's grave. She reached up and brushed a finger across Brody's face. It came away damp, and to her surprise, his mouth lifted at the edges.

"One day soon, we need to talk." He pressed a kiss to the back of her hand. "Will you do something for me?"

"Anything."

"Sit with the other children for a spell? It won't be much longer."

20

WINDOWS RATTLED YET stood strong against the fierce wind. Raindrops assailed the glass and beat down on the roof, and all the while, the only sounds echoing from within the clinic came from the parents and siblings of Otto Rowland.

An hour after Katharine brought the children into their youngest brother's room, she sat next to Brody at the long table in the center of his kitchen. The rich coffee, now cold, sat untouched next to the uneaten food Tilly had brought over from the café. The occasional sob or soft crying split through the silence on the lower floor.

"What will happen to the other two boys?"

"Their fevers broke. I'll watch them for a few more days, but if they don't worsen, they should be all right." Brody rested his forearms on the table and watched the rain fall through a window. "This weather will delay your people's departure."

"Stewart and Bessie said again that they won't leave until I do."

Brody shifted in his seat and rested one arm on the back of the chair so he could look at her. "Your father will no doubt send someone to at least assure himself you are well. Telegrams or no, he must worry when you're apart."

"This is the first time I can recall . . . Do you hear that, Finn?"

"I hear it." He was on his feet and headed toward the rear kitchen entrance before

Katharine pushed her chair back. He slid the wooden crossbar left and eased the door open while pressing against the force of the wind. Soaked through and wrapped in a blanket, Mary lay unconscious in Colton's arms.

"Good God, man!"

Colton transferred Mary to Brody's arms. "We got another one, Doc."

Brody carried Mary with as much care as possible into the surgery. He heard Katharine's cry and a few seconds later Colton and Gabriel half-dragged Ethan into the room.

Brody lifted Mary again and motioned to the table. "Put him there. I'll be right back." He carried Mary into his bedroom and laid her gently on the bed. Katharine followed.

Brody unwrapped Mary from the blanket. His stomach tightened at the sight of fresh bruises.

Katharine reached out a hand, then pulled it back. "What can I do to help?"

He wished he could spare her, but he recognized his own inability to care for so many patients at once. He quickly checked Mary and found no bleeding except from scrapes and cuts. "I'll see what happened to Ethan and then I'll return." Brody covered Mary with the quilt from his bed. "Sit with her only, Kate. I won't be long."

"What happened?" Brody strode across the room to the examination table where Ethan lay awake and clutched his arm close to his body.

"It's not a fatal wound, Doc. See to the girl."

Brody, being one of only two other men in the room as big as Ethan Gallagher, pushed the man back down. "You'll stay until I have a look. How did this happen, and where did you find Mary?"

Colton wiped water from his face and stood a few feet away from the table. "I went back out after Ethan spoke with Katharine. I found her running barefoot, in a nightgown, a few miles south of the mine."

"Did Mary say anything?"

Colton secured the damp hat back on his head. "She screamed at first, probably thinking I was one of the men who . . . I stopped my horse, and she kept running. She slipped in the mud and after that was unconscious."

With skilled fingers, Brody examined the wound. "This is from a blade, and a big one."

"An unexpected ambush." Ethan grit his teeth. "Gabriel and I went back out after Ben and I checked in at the ranch."

Gabriel said, "The bastard threw the

knife. With the rain, none of us saw it coming. We found Colton heading back here. How bad is it, Doc?"

"Not fatal, as Ethan said. What happened to your assailant?"

"Gabriel got off a shot, but we didn't find the guy."

Brody motioned Gabriel over. "Help me get his shirt off. I'll need you sitting upright for this part, Ethan." Brody held a light close to the exit on Ethan's upper back where it came through his shoulder. "I won't know for sure until I get in there for a better look, but from the way you're *not* moving your arm, I'd say the knife sliced through some muscle."

"Stitch it up, Brody. Brenna will have all our hides if I don't come back tonight."

"She'd rather have you safe here than bleeding out on the road home." Brody pressed a cloth to the back of the wound and helped Ethan lie back down so the pressure from his own body helped stop the bleeding. He placed another cloth on the entry wound. "Hold this here. I need to clean the wound properly, and then I'll stitch it up."

"I can wait." Ethan pointed to the other room. "Help her first."

An argument would just waste time, so Brody agreed and left Gabriel and Colton to keep Ethan in line until he returned.

Brody stopped outside the bedroom when he heard Katharine's soft and lyrical voice. It took him a moment to recognize the words from the old Irish ballad, "She Is Far from the Land," a melancholy song that conjured memories of home and the love and lives torn apart by war.

"You have the voice of a lark." He draped a towel near the foot of the bed.

"It was all I could think of."

"Where did you learn that song?" Brody checked Mary's pulse and found it strong.

"My father sang it to me all the time after my mother died." Katharine smoothed a damp cloth over Mary's brow. "How badly do you think she is hurt?"

"I won't know until the examination."

"You hinted before that you have treated a woman before, who suffered as Mary has."

Brody did his best to block out the memories from the war, but it did not take much to bring them to the surface. "She was a young widow, about Mary's age. The war was three years in, and I swear madness took over too many of the men. A cousin who came to visit found the woman and her daughter in their home, a nearby plantation. The doctor with whom I was apprenticing was her regular physician, but he was out when two of her servants brought her in."

"Did she live?"

"The mother did, for a short while." He lifted the lower half of the quilt and left only her feet and legs exposed. These he covered with a towel and rubbed the extremities. "It's time for you to leave the room, Kate."

"I want to help." She dropped the damp cloth in a bowl and stood.

He met her bold stare with one of his own. Brody shifted his focus back to the patient. "We'll need warm water, and more on the kettle to boil, and a clean nightgown if you can find one." Brody grabbed her arm before she moved away. "Once those tasks are seen to, I need you to stay out of the room. Please."

Katharine hesitated long enough for Brody to ask her again. This time she agreed. "I will check on Ethan."

Colton stepped into the room but stayed by the door. "I'll take care of the water if you get the nightgown."

At Katharine's nod, Colton went to fetch the water, and she returned a short while later with a new nightgown from the mercantile. For the next two hours, Brody moved from one patient to the next. He had not seen Katharine in the past hour, but he did not regret sending her away while he completed his examination. This time, at least, she had not suffered the same abuse.

Mary would have to find an incredible amount of inner strength to survive the coming days and weeks, maybe years. The young widow he'd treated gave up the fight after someone told her the men had done the same thing to her daughter. Brody could heal her physical injuries, but only Mary could choose to live and eventually overcome what they had inflicted on her. The emotional scars would be deeper.

Pain shrouded over more than one room in the clinic, a grief so great there would be no full recovery. Brody stood outside Otto Rowland's room and listened to his parents' murmured prayer and his siblings' soft cries. Katharine stood in a corner close to the porch, and after the prayer finished, she silently stepped outside. Brody left the family to say their goodbyes in private.

A hard pounding on the front door preceded the portal opening and voices carried into the room. Brody stepped into the hall and resigned himself to a confrontation. At least he wouldn't be the one to receive a lashing.

"Eliza."

She halted mid-stride, with Ramsey one step behind. Eliza ignored the drops of water falling from her coat to the floor below. "Where are those fool brothers of mine?"

21

ETHAN SAT UP with his injured shoulder in a white, cloth sling and held up a hand before Eliza could speak.

"What in the hell are you doing out in this storm?"

Eliza closed the space between her and Ethan, while Ramsey wisely leaned against the wall and waited. He shrugged when Ethan glanced his way.

"I've ridden in worse, but at least I have the sense not to go looking for trouble in it." She lightly punched her brother's good arm and then hugged him. "Ben told us where you went." She looked over her shoulder at Brody. "You sure he's all right?"

Brody held his smile in check. "Punching doesn't help."

Eliza narrowed her eyes.

"He'll be fine, but he can't use the arm for a few weeks. This isn't the first time he's injured that shoulder." Brody walked over to his patient. "How's the pain?"

"I've had worse, and whatever you gave me has helped." Ethan slid off the table onto his long legs and reached for his shirt. "No way can I go weeks without using the arm."

"Your arm, your choice, but I'll ignore my oath as a doctor and leave you to fend for yourself if you're too stubborn to let the shoulder heal properly." He stepped aside so Eliza could help her brother into his shirt. She glared at him all while buttoning it.

"Did you tell Brenna where we went?"

Eliza gave him a look that said, "What do you think?"

"Right. As soon as the storm lets up, we're heading back to the ranch. I'll explain what happened, and then Ramsey, I'd appreciate it if you let Tom know the other guy didn't make it."

Ramsey moved from his spot against the wall. "The guy who cut you?" He pointed to Ethan's injury.

"Yeah, him."

Silence filled the room when one by one the occupants faced the doorway. Brody walked to Katharine and spoke softly for her hearing only. "You were there when Otto passed."

"It happened so fast, Finn. One minute he seemed better, and then the next he was gone. Do you think he suffered?"

"No." At his parents' request, Brody had given the boy just enough morphine to dull any pain. They had already known their son was slipping away. "Did you just come from their room?"

"Yes. Ada refuses to let go of her son's hand, and I understand her grief, but she speaks as if he is only sleeping."

"She understands he's gone, Kate. It will take time."

"The rain is letting up. If there is somewhere to take the boy . . ." Katharine peered around him at the others, remembering they were not alone. "How are you, Ethan?"

"Well enough for any more time to be spent hovering over me. How is Mary?"

Brody took over answering. "She has a long road to recovery, though we still aren't certain that's her name. Katharine, you haven't yet met Eliza Cameron."

Katharine accepted the other woman's hand in friendship. "I wish it could be under different circumstances."

"People usually find themselves where they're meant to be at the time." No one else thought Eliza's cryptic response odd, so Katharine said nothing more.

Brody said to Ethan, "You're going to leave whether or not I tell you to stay, so go, but I expect all of you to make sure he gets home without opening his wound." No one verbally accepted responsibility. Brody started for the door with Katharine when Eliza called his name. "I'm not here just to yell at my brothers." She spoke to Brody but looked at Gabriel. "Isabelle is fine, but she was complaining of pains. Elizabeth gave her some of the tea you left on the last visit, but it doesn't seem to help."

Gabriel grabbed his coat and hat. Eliza clasped his arm. "She's fine, and she didn't even ask for a doctor. Elizabeth just thought it might help if he can check on Isabelle tomorrow, but she's fine." She looked then at Brody. "You've got a lot going on here."

"Tell Isabelle I will be there in the morning." This time he left the room and with his hand on Katharine's back, gave her no choice but to go with him. When they were reasonably alone, he said, "You asked about moving the boy. I have a room attached to the clinic where I ready bodies for burial, but I don't want to move Otto there yet. It will be better for Ada if she leaves the room on her own. I'll go up there now."

Katharine held fast to his hand when he would have moved away. She wrapped her arms around him and leaned against his chest, surprising him enough into automatically responding to her embrace. "Give yourself a minute, Finn."

He did. A slow breath in and another out, over and over until his body relaxed.

"It never ends, does it?"

Brody rested his cheek against the top of her head. "There is always a need for healing." He held her until they heard the others moving down the hall, and she slipped from his embrace. They simultaneously glanced toward the window where enough light remained in the sky to make moving about doable. "The rain has stopped. I will see about food for everyone and then sit with Mary."

"Kate." He wasn't ready to let her go yet knew he must. Brody released her and went to tend to his patients.

———✦———

Katharine awakened to a thin strip of sunlight making its way into the room through a half-open curtain. She closed her eyes again, then opened them one at a time as they adjusted to the light. She did not recognize the bed beneath her or the room in which she had slept, but for how long?

Katharine lifted her from beneath a pillow and saw she wore one of her lace-trimmed, cotton nightgowns, though she had no recollection of how she came to wear it or how she came to be in bed.

A soft, familiar humming gave her hope she was somewhere she should be, and Katharine slowly sat up and inspected her surroundings.

"You're awake." Bessie laid out a clean skirt and blouse and all the undergarments.

"Bessie." She pushed back the covers and left the comfort of the bed. "How did I get here?"

"Your friend, Doctor Brody, should not be so familiar with you, Miss Katharine."

"What do you disapprove of Bessie?"

"He carried you over here last night, for all to see."

Katharine recalled sitting with Mary after fetching the food. She remembered nothing after. "I must have been exhausted not to have woken."

Bessie "tsked" and clucked her tongue as she poured water from a ceramic pitcher into a large, white bowl. "You were awake long enough to help me change you into your nightclothes. Have you decided on a change in profession?"

Not at all in good enough spirits to deal with Bessie's censure, she crossed the room to the bowl of water and gently splashed some on her face. She searched and found a small clock on the bureau. It read half-past eight o'clock in the morning, which meant she'd been away from the clinic . . . "What time did the doctor bring me here?"

"Around ten o'clock."

Bessie set out a pair of dainty boots made of soft, kid leather.

"The front-laced boots today, Bessie. I have a bit of walking to do. Where is Stewart?"

Her maid's pinched lips attested to further disapproval. "He is having breakfast at the café."

"Have you had yours yet?"

Bessie shook her head and found the boots Katharine wanted from the trunk.

"Go then and enjoy your breakfast. I can manage."

"But, Miss, you still need to get dressed."

"The clothes I need today are simple enough."

Bessie gave a few last tugs at the edges of

the skirt and blouse before leaving the room. Katharine sighed and removed her nightgown and indulged in a thorough sponge bath before cleaning her teeth. Donning the petticoats and chemise were easy, and the corset buttoned in front. She did not bother trying to tighten the strings and breathed easier for it.

Once dressed, her hair was another matter and made her acknowledge how much she had always relied on Bessie for even the simplest of tasks. She piled the thick locks loosely on top of her head and poked more pins in there than Bessie would have. The careless result would suffice for what she had planned for the day.

With hat in hand, Katharine left the room and went in search of Mr. Baker, who she found cleaning a glass countertop in the store. "Good Morning, Mr. Baker."

"Call me, Loren. Did you sleep all right? You looked half-dead when Doc brought you over last night."

Speaking to the good doctor about that was next on her list of tasks. "I did, thank you. Your hospitality for me and my travel companions has been most appreciated."

Loren shrugged. "It's what we do."

"How is Joanna?"

"Ornery." Loren chuckled and looked upward. "Don't go telling her I said so. She wants to get back to work, but Doc told her she has to stay in bed a couple more days."

"Doctor Brody was here this morning?"

Loren nodded and returned the duster to a drawer. "Stopped by for a few supplies before heading out to Hawk's Peak. Didn't say why, though."

Katharine remembered Eliza mentioning Isabelle, who she recalled was with child. "I see. Well, I shall visit with

Joanna once I conclude my business for the day."

"She'd sure appreciate the company. Bessie reads to her some, been a real help."

A trace of guilt reminded Katharine of her brusque behavior with Bessie earlier. "I am pleased. Would you—"

A sharp and insistent knock at the door of the general store had Loren rounding the counter and pulling back the curtain to see who stood on the other side. He opened the portal without hesitation. "It's mighty early to see you in town, Eliza."

Eliza greeted Loren with a hug and an inquiry after Joanna's health, when she added, "I'm here to see Miss Kiely." Eliza gave her attention to Katharine. "We have some business at the land office."

"Where's Ethan?"

Eliza grinned. "Brenna refused to let him

ride again until Brody cleared him, and Gabriel is with Isabelle. The doc arrived as Ramsey and I were leaving." They said goodbye to Loren, and Katharine followed Eliza outside. The crisp, cool air filled her lungs, and the quiet street beckoned them to step down from the boardwalk.

"There isn't much activity out here."

Eliza waved to Orin who stood outside the small land office. "A lot of folks are cleaning up after the storm. Downed trees and some damaged roofs will keep people busy for a few days. Those without cleanup will help others." They stopped in the middle of the road. "My brothers trust you, so I'm going to trust you meant what you told them . . . that you have no intention of building a spur line for the mine."

"I meant it, and while I still think it would benefit the town, your family's position is understandable."

"Then what's all this about needing to look at the original land documents?"

Katharine took the lead this time and closed the rest of the distance to the land office. Orin smiled at them both and unlocked the door. "We are about to find out."

22

KATHARINE SHUFFLED THROUGH the land certificates for the acreage under scrutiny while Orin Lloyd opened two more drawers in search of the correct map.

"I think . . ." He pulled out a thick roll and bent to pick up a sheet of paper that fluttered to the wood floor. "Hmm." He studied the sheet of paper, half unrolled the maps, and nodded. "Yes, it should be here." Orin spread them out on the tall table in the center of the room. Katharine held down one end while Eliza looked it over.

"This is the right one." Eliza pointed out the area the mine wanted the spur line to run through. "This is the original survey my father had done when he bought the land."

Katharine studied the certificate, which listed 160 acres, and turned back to the survey map. "Is this area still empty?"

"No." Eliza ran a finger along the east boundary line. "This is where the edge of town begins."

"Has the railroad ever offered to buy your land?"

Eliza shook her head. "No need. It's good acreage, but they'd have no reason to invest in a rail to Briarwood. They've put their resources to reaching areas with more growth. There's Jameston's mine, but it's a minor operation compared to others in the area."

Katharine looked up at Orin. "Is there a magnifying glass in here?"

"Think so." He opened another drawer

and pulled one out. "Here you go."

She thanked him and held it over the area on the other side of the Gallaghers' land. "This is an interesting boundary line. It follows a path similar to a stream, but I don't remember seeing one on any of the maps we have."

"You wouldn't have. That section dried up a decade ago, after it was rerouted into the creek flowing through the meadow. It occasionally fills with rain, but it's mostly rock bed now." Eliza raised a brow. "What are you thinking?"

"Well, this land here," Katharine pointed to the land on the other side of the stream. "Who owns it?"

"It's still government land. Why?"

Katharine held the magnifying glass over the edge of the map. "Your land does not appear to be the best route for a spur line if the mine is the destination. See here? This is the new branch off the main line from Butte. If they built the spur from here," she pointed to a section on the federal land, "then they'd have a more direct route to the main line. It would be easier to buy federal land than to fight over yours, and they wouldn't have to wait until someone builds new lines through the territory."

Orin hovered near both of them. "Well, I'll be."

Eliza asked, "We can count on your discretion, Orin?"

"Yes, ma'am. I'm bound to keep your confidence."

"Only for mail and telegrams, Orin."

The tall man stood straight. "You can count on my discretion." He tapped the papers. "But I can't let you leave with those."

"If there is blank paper and something to

write with, I can make some notes." Orin handed her a sheet of paper from a small stack on a shelf and a slate pencil from his own pocket. He watched over her shoulder as she drew the general boundary lines of the Gallaghers' land, the dried-up stream, and the federal land. She marked the point for the mine location and the town and handed the pencil back. "Thank you, Orin. You have been a great help."

"Oh, almost forgot, Miss Kiely." Orin patted his vest and removed a small, folded piece of paper. "This telegram came last night for you."

Katharine unfolded the paper and read the short telegram to herself.

Want details on project cancellation and trust your judgment -(STOP)- Please notify me when you will return home -(STOP)- New project to commence in Utah next month.

Eliza joined her a few minutes later out front and waited for Orin to lock the office and leave. "Are you all right?"

"What?" Katharine tucked the telegram away. "Yes, fine. A wire from my father. He wants details on why I cancelled the project."

"Seems you have more questions than before."

Katharine nodded. "I want to know more for myself, to know if I acted hastily or if there is merit to my suspicions."

"Ethan said you thought Jameston might want the land for another purpose."

"I still do. My surveyor and his assistants walked the property for two days and said nothing stood out, but he focused on the section where the spur would travel." Katharine looked up and down the street and saw the small town was busier than a short while ago. "I want to stop at the clinic, and then if you will allow me, I would like to look over your parcel of land."

"Brenna said you handled a horse well enough. It will be easier and faster to ride than walk."

Katharine wasn't so sure about that but agreed.

"I'll get you a horse from the livery and meet you at the clinic. I need to let Ramsey know what we're doing. He's at the sheriff's office."

"Is everything all right?"

"It is now. He helped Tom mediate a skirmish between two farmers south of town." Eliza crossed the road, said hello to a few people along the way, and disappeared into the sheriff's office, where she assumed they also kept the jail.

Five minutes later, Katharine was upstairs at the clinic, surprised to see Brody in the room with Mary. "I thought you were at Hawk's Peak. You must have raced the horse the whole way to be back already."

Brody nodded and stepped just out of the room so they could speak. "It wasn't anything serious, but Isabelle will need to be on bed rest for a few weeks." He scrubbed a hand over his face. "I'm surprised to see you this early."

"I was at the land office with Eliza. We're going out for a ride shortly, but I wanted to check in on Mary. Any change?"

"None."

"It's quiet. Where are the Rowlands?"

"They left after breakfast. Ada didn't want to stay in the place where her son died. I don't blame her for leaving, though I would have liked to monitor the other two boys for a few more days." Brody leaned the full length of his back against the hallway wall. "Otto is downstairs. The service is this afternoon."

"How do you keep him . . . never mind."

"Ice."

Katharine tried to block the sudden image from her mind. She instead wrapped her arms around him in a move that was becoming habit, and Brody held her close. "Will you be going to the funeral?" She felt his nod against the top of her head. "You carried me to bed last night?" The sentence came out far more intimate than she intended. "I mean—"

He tilted her head back as a finger brushed over her cheek. "I know what you meant," he said scant seconds before he pressed his lips to hers. The heady kiss was more than Katharine expected, and shock did not have time to cloud her judgment when she leaned into the embrace.

A low moan ended the kiss too quickly. Brody gently moved her aside and rushed into the bedroom. Mary saw them both and tears immediately flowed from terrified eyes. "No. No, no, no."

Brody did not go to her side, and reading the situation, Katharine sat on the edge of the bed. "It's all right, Mary. You're safe here."

She shook her head. "Mary. Not Mary. She's . . . water." She choked out the last word and tried to raise her head.

Katharine lifted the half-full water glass from off the bedside table and held it against the other woman's lips. She drank most of the water before pressing her head back into the pillow. "Your name isn't Mary?"

"Sister," she whispered. "My sister is Mary."

Katharine looked up at Brody, then back at the patient. "Was Mary with you?"

She nodded this time. "Have to find her."

"What's your name, lass?"

"Rachel." Her eyes rolled back, and her entire body shook.

"Finn!"

"I've got her." He moved Katharine away and held Rachel still until the shaking subsided. He checked first a pulse, then her breathing. "She's all right. Rachel, can you hear me?"

She emitted a soft moan and twisted away from Brody. "They have her."

"Rachel." Katharine leaned close and spoke in hushed tones. "Can you hear us?" She started in on the song she was singing earlier, and with each line, Rachel's body relaxed a little more. She finally opened her eyes again and looked directly at them.

"That's right." Brody approached her again, slowly. "Nod if you understand me."

Rachel nodded the best she could manage.

"Good. You had a seizure, Rachel."

Katharine and Brody both heard the door open downstairs, and the doctor's name called out. It sounded like Eliza, but she heard more than one person walking around. "I'll go."

Rachel grasped her arm as she moved away. Brody squeezed Katharine's shoulder and whispered close to her ear. "You stay."

When Brody left the room, Katharine searched for the right words to say, uncertain there could be any for such a situation. Her sheltered life had always been a fact of her upbringing, and she at times resented it. Now, gratitude overwhelmed her for the safety her father provided, even as sorrow cut through and brought reality to the forefront.

"Rachel, I promise from this moment forward, you will be safe."

"The others."

The constriction in Katharine's chest hit her with a jolt. "What others?"

"In the wagon. There were five—" Rachel's head rolled to the side as once again she passed out.

23

"SHE TOLD US her sister was with her. Her *sister* is Mary. Her name is Rachel."

"There are more."

Brody turned at the sound of footsteps on the staircase. "What did she tell you?"

"Five women in the wagon is what she said before she passed out." Katharine brushed her fingers over Brody's arm. "She's sleeping. What would have caused her seizure?"

"A head injury or other trauma is most likely, considering what she has been through. If it was a regular condition like epilepsy, she would have presented the first time she was here."

Ramsey took over the questioning. "Cletus Drake told you he didn't see anyone else when he first found her, correct?"

"Yes. It's possible she escaped the first time as well. She wouldn't have survived this long, with what she's endured, if she wasn't strong, but it's hard to believe she would have left a sister behind." Brody considered all the scenarios in which a wagon filled with women would have been driving toward Briarwood. He heard the stories of young women forced to work at brothels, but never around here, and if the others were like Rachel, with fine clothing and smooth hands, the entire situation made little sense. "Colton said he tracked the man who took Rachel back to the mining camp, but then there was no sign of any women. Do you know if they checked the houses where the married men and their families live?"

"There wouldn't have been a reason to, Brody." Ramsey glanced at his wife. "And Jameston will not let us back up there. It's private land, and he's been as cooperative as he's going to be, especially after Ethan and Gabriel's last visit. I'll need cause, or permission from a judge, and one will not give that without a witness or proof of wrongdoing. Rachel needs to give us more information. In the meantime, I have a friend in the Pinkerton Agency. The reality is, these women may not even be in the territory any longer, and the Pinkertons are better equipped to investigate."

Disheartened, Katharine asked, "You're going to stop looking?"

"No." Ramsey secured his hat in place and handed Eliza's to her while she put her long duster back on. "We're going to do all we can, but we need Rachel to talk to us.

When the Pinkerton gets here—Julian Frank—he's going to need to speak with her as well." "She trusts you." Brody looked upward at the sound of Rachel's voice. "And she's awake again."

"Of course." Katharine started for the stairs again. "But perhaps just Ramsey. You can relay what you learn to your friend."

Eliza and Brody agreed to wait downstairs, and Ramsey followed Katharine to the second level. Rachel was pushing herself into a sitting position. Her wary gaze fastened onto Ramsey as he walked into the room and put a little distance between himself and the bed.

"Rachel." Katharine sat in the chair she'd left near the bed earlier. "This is Ramsey Cameron. He has a friend who may be able to help find your sister and the other women you spoke of, but you need to tell him what you remember."

Rachel's voice was clear when she spoke. "Do you trust him?"

"With my life. He's a friend of the doctor who saved your life."

Rachel fidgeted with the ends of the sheet, with her gaze downward. "I need to apologize to the doctor. I wasn't kind earlier."

Katharine held the other woman's hand to offer whatever comfort it might give. "He understands."

"It started in San Francisco." Rachel inhaled a shuddering breath and squeezed Katharine's fingers. "Mary and I worked in a wealthy household. I was a governess, and she was a housemaid. We always had dreams for glorious adventures. We'd never been anywhere outside the city, and the son of the man we worked for traveled all over. He told amazing tales and . . ."

Ramsey searched the room and carried a pitcher of water over to Katharine, who refilled Rachel's glass. After a few drinks, Rachel continued. "Mary never wanted to be a maid, and she begged me to go with her." She raised her tear-stained face, and this time looked directly at Ramsey. "You see, she answered an advertisement that promised introductions to eligible men in the Rocky Mountains who were searching for wives."

"Did you answer one of these advertisements?"

"No! No." Rachel lifted the end of the sheet and then paused in raising the sleeve of her nightgown. Anticipating her need, Katharine withdrew one of her own fine linen handkerchiefs and handed it to Rachel. "Thank you. No, I promised Mary I would travel with her, but then I intended to return to San Francisco. My job was a good one, and I was always more of a dreamer than a doer."

Katharine saw the toll the conversation was taking on Rachel. "We can stop if you need to rest."

She dabbed the cloth around her nose and mouth but watched Ramsey. "You need more, don't you?"

Ramsey pointed to the bed. "May I come a little closer?"

Rachel did not answer right away. She stared at Ramsey like prey does when faced by an unexpected attack from a hunter . . . do they flee or stand still and hope the hunter moves on? Finally, she nodded once.

Ramsey took two steps forward and no more. "As much as you can remember."

"Do you think you can find my sister?"

"I won't make a promise I can't keep . . . may I call you Rachel?"

"Yes. It's Rachel Watson."

Ramsey acknowledged and said, "I've already told Katharine and Doctor Brody this, but the reality of your sister, or the other women, still being in the territory are not good. Since you first got away, they've had plenty of time to get them out if they suspected you talked to anyone about what happened."

Rachel darted glances between Katharine and Ramsey. "I didn't get away the first time."

Katharine leaned closer. "How then were you found?"

"Found?"

Ramsey explained, "A trapper who comes through the area sometimes found you outside of town. You were alone, and there was no sign of anyone else around. We thought you escaped."

Rachel appeared to consider her words,

and as the seconds ticked by, her upper body shivered. "I don't remember how or . . . I remember what he did." Rachel squeezed her eyes closed.

"You don't have to say anything about that." Katharine shot Ramsey a look she hoped made him understand he needed to change the direction of his questions.

"My apologies, Rachel." Ramsey gave her a minute before asking, "Do you want to stop?"

Rachel pounded a fist on her leg. "No! I want to finish. I need to find my sister. We traveled by train for as long as we could, and then in Butte there were four other women, all well-dressed. They were all so excited, and then . . . it all went wrong. Mary overhead the couple traveling with us. Mary didn't say *what* she heard because everything after that happened so fast."

"Wait," Ramsey interrupted. "You were traveling with a couple? A man and woman?"

"Yes. They were maybe ten years older than you."

Katharine asked, "Where are your parents?"

"Gone." Rachel covered her light whimper behind the handkerchief. "It has been only Mary and me for three years."

Ramsey took one more step closer to the bed. "What does all this have to do with the mine?"

"Mine?"

Katharine drew her attention. "You don't remember being at the mine? Or a Mr. Jameston?"

"Jameston," Rachel murmured. "He was a nice man. We met him in Butte."

Eliza pulled herself up and into the saddle. "It will be an hour or more before Gabriel and Colton arrive. They can meet us out there."

Without siblings herself, Katharine wondered how Eliza knew her brothers so well, and how she was so sure Colton would join him. "Not Ethan?"

She grinned. "He'll stay behind to pacify Brenna." Eliza said to Brody, "If anyone can convince my brother to rest for a few days, it's her."

"I'm counting on it." Brody helped Katharine onto the mare Eliza borrowed for her from the livery and then got comfortable atop his gelding. He refused to let her go without him, though he kept his reasons to himself.

Rachel slept after the emotional retelling of what happened, and Flora promised to look in. Brody could not put off the search for a nurse any longer. Most days he could handle the few cases that arose, but as the territory and town continued to grow, he would not be able to keep up on his own.

Stewart, on one of the horses they used to pull the supply wagon, rounded the corner. Katharine called out a greeting and then told the others, "Stewart reads maps and landscapes better than anyone I know."

"I have a telegram to send, and then I'll catch up with you." Ramsey leaned over and whispered something to his wife, then led his horse the short distance to Orin's telegraph office.

Forty minutes later, Stewart brought the party to a halt. He held the copied map steady in front of him, studied the surroundings, and confirmed. "This is the place, Miss Kiely."

"You're certain?"

Eliza rode up alongside Stewart and looked across at the map. "May I?" Stewart handed the document over. "We haven't walked this land in years, but I remember a small cave near here. It wasn't deep, maybe ten feet." Eliza pointed to a general area of the map. "Somewhere around here. Gabe or Colton will know better. I'm sure it's used by trappers or hunters from time to time. We're here now, Katharine. What is it you think we'll find?"

Katharine slid off the back of the horse, having sat in sidesaddle fashion to accommodate her skirt. Her body jarred when her feet hit the ground, and she remained upright thanks to Brody, who somehow reached her side before she realized he was there. "I need practice."

The horse offered them some privacy, and Katharine had to walk around the front to see Eliza. "The land in this region is rich in gold, copper, and silver, yes?"

"It is, mostly silver and copper these days, but you can't just walk along and see mineral veins. It takes some work." Eliza also climbed down from her horse. "If someone had found gold in the old stream bed, we would have heard about it. What made you think there'd be anything to find?"

"Other than Jameston's reaction, we had something similar on a Colorado project. An opposing party to the spur line found gold, and I thought—"

"Wait." Eliza asked for the map from Stewart. "You might not be wrong."

"What do you mean?"

"The mine owns this land north, and the mine entrance is close to the boundary line. It's possible—"

The map landed on the dirt and rocks

with a hole through the center.

"Get down!" Brody yanked Katharine close to him and shielded her until he pushed her behind a nearby tree. "Eliza!"

24

"I'm all right!" Brody saw Eliza duck behind a rock, and his visual search of Stewart showed the older man lying flat on the hard ground.

"Can you see if they hit him?"

"Don't move, Kate." Brody stood up as much as he could to see, but the tree did not completely hide him from the shooters. "He's breathing." He hunched low again and brushed Katharine's fallen hair from her face. "Are you all right?"

Her rapid breathing slowed. "Yes. Has the shooting stopped?"

Brody pointed to her hat. "May I have that?"

She didn't ask him why. Katharine removed the pin and passed him her hat. Brody dropped two small rocks into the crown and tossed it as one would a plate into the air. It didn't go far, but far enough for another bullet to destroy it.

"My rifle is still in the scabbard." Brody assessed the immediate surroundings and saw little more than trees like the one concealing them. "I don't see them out there. They have the high ground, and more cover, which means Eliza won't be able to get a shot with her pistol."

"I'm smaller. What if I crawled low to—"

"Not as long as I'm breathing." Brody raised a hand and immediately drew it back. A bullet landed in a tree behind them. "They aren't going anywhere."

"Brody!"

"Here." He sneaked a quick look and saw Eliza hadn't moved, and she kept one of her legs straight as she shifted her position.

"You remember the hunting trip you went on with Gabe and Ethan last year?"

Brody held a finger up to his lips to signal Katharine not to speak. "I remember."

"Ethan told me how you met up with a sow and her cubs on the last day. I wanted to kill Gabe when he laughed later about how you all got away."

"Getting away from the grizzly was easier." Brody got as low to the ground as possible and peered around the base of the trunk again, keeping Katharine in place with his body so he could get a better look at Eliza. She sat with her back against the boulder and crouched low enough so her head remained below the top. Her riding skirt was torn halfway up the right leg and Brody caught sight of a thin stream of blood on her skin. He waited for her to look at him before inching back.

Katharine said, "I assume neither of you cares about the bear story."

Brody smiled for her benefit. "No, but it might get us out of here, or distract these guys long enough for the others to arrive."

"How can you be sure they are coming?"

"Ramsey said they would." Brody gathered a handful of rocks and placed them in a small pile. "No matter what happens, I want you to stay here."

"Why? Where are you going?"

Brody kissed her hard and fast. "Trust me." He glimpsed Eliza's horse and saw the rifle still in its scabbard. He hurled three of the small rocks into the air and far to the right, then another two to the left. Shots from the trees quickly followed, and Brody sent three more rocks in quick succession toward the shooters as he ran out from behind the tree. Eliza fired her pistol at the same time, one shot after another, until she drew their fire away from Brody.

Every instinct in him shouted for him to stop and check on Stewart, who had not moved since they fired the first shots, but there was more than one life at stake. The unmistakable sound of an empty chamber filled the air, and the shooters redirected their attention to Brody, who pulled the rifle out and smacked the horse on the rump before ducking behind another tree. He had more cover from this vantage point, but still did not see a target. He fired one shot into the general direction of the earlier ones. This time, no one returned fire.

"Eliza!"

Shouts from down the road propelled Brody around. He fired one more warning shot into the trees and heard nothing in return. Brody ran across the short distance and skid to his knees in front of Stewart. He glimpsed a white petticoat as Katharine used the tree to help her stand. "Stay there, Kate!"

He checked the neck and wrist for a pulse and pressed his ear to the man's chest to listen for any sound of a heartbeat. Brody swore for his ears only and ignored the discord around him as Gabriel hugged and yelled at Eliza simultaneously. Ramsey swept Eliza into his arms and carried her to where Brody still knelt next to Stewart.

He remembered Eliza's injury and drew his attention to where it needed to be. "My medical supplies are in my saddle bags."

"I'll find your horse," Gabriel said and clamped him on the shoulder before leaving.

"Were you shot?"

Eliza's jaw tightened against the pain of Brody's probing fingers. "No, I fell against a sharp rock when the shooting started. It's a scratch."

"This is more than a scratch, Eliza." Brody opened the medical bag Gabriel set next to him and pulled out a bandage, folded it twice, and pressed it against the source of the bleeding. "Ramsey, hold this in place. Eliza, I'm going to secure the bandage, but I want to stitch you up at the clinic. Gabriel, we're going to need a wagon. She can't ride."

Gabriel tugged on his sister's finger. "Eliza—"

"Don't. You and Ethan can yell at me later, when you're together and after I take whatever Doc gives me for the pain."

Gabriel got to his feet and without a word, swung up onto the back of his horse and road toward town.

"Brody?"

Brody looked up and Katharine approached, for there was no obvious reason she should remain hidden any longer, except his deep desire to protect her as she dropped next to Stewart's body.

"No. Please, God, no." She raised tear-filled eyes, but Brody did not have to speak aloud what she already knew.

He met Eliza's gaze, saw her nod, and leaving Ramsey to temporarily look after his wife, Brody moved to the other side of Stewart and held Katharine in his arms while she wept.

———⊰⊱———

A soft rain accompanied young Otto Rowland's burial. Even the birds and wind accepted the solemn intrusion into their world and remained still and silent as the softest beads of water dropped from a sun-kissed halo in the sky.

All those in attendance held their heads low as Reverend Phillips prayed, with the mourning broken only by the boy's mother, who reached for the small coffin even as her husband held her close.

No one in Briarwood, save the few who helped during the children's illness, knew the young family, and yet all who were able had shown up for the service. Ethan, his arm still in a sling, stood next to Brenna and Gabriel. Next to him stood Ramsey and Amanda, and beside her was an older woman Katharine did not recognize. Eliza, unable to walk yet, remained at the clinic, and Katharine shouldered the burden of responsibility for that as well. Now, as the gathering dispersed, Denny and Ada Rowland, with their three, remaining offspring, moved closer to the coffin.

Brody walked beside Katharine away from the cemetery, and every step led her both farther and closer to death, for with one funeral over, another needed to be planned. It was she who stopped and watched the family. "Bessie wants her brother returned to Astoria."

"I cannot prepare his body to allow that distance of travel."

Katharine averted her gaze from the Rowlands and walked again toward town. "There is nothing we can do?"

"There is an embalmer in Bozeman. I can send word and ask him to come, but it may be . . ." Brody tugged gently on her arm. "You have said little since we returned to town yesterday."

"You were busy with Eliza, and then Ada wasn't ready to bury her son yet, and

Stewart . . . I have known him more than half my life." Katharine changed direction and cut a path across an expanse of dirt and light grass to stand near a stone cottage. "What purpose did any of it serve? They killed Stewart for what? Why? So I could validate my assumptions and suspicions about Jameston? I already decided not to work the man, so why did I pursue it? Stewart did not understand, but he followed direction like always." She fought the tightness in her chest. "My father would have managed the situation with far more skill."

"Come, sit here." Brody stepped onto the narrow porch and lowered himself onto the bench.

"I will not avail myself of someone else's porch."

He held out his hand. "The cottage belongs to the Gallaghers, and it is rarely in use. They won't mind us sitting for a few minutes."

She accepted his offer and sat next to him. "Do you think they already left?"

"They'll take a meal at Tilly's and visit with folks in town before looking in on Eliza. They rarely get into town, except one or two at a time. Eliza has already said she wants to go home and recuperate there. It's almost impossible to keep those three still for long."

Katharine assumed he referred to Ethan, Gabriel, and Eliza, and after the short time in their company, she thought it could be true. She remembered the older woman. "Who stood next to Amanda at the service?"

"Elizabeth, grandmother to Ramsey and Brenna. She has a fair hand at healing herself and tends to those at the ranch when they have smaller mishaps. She's proven to be a talented midwife, too, and it comforts some women to have her close during a birthing." Brody kissed the top of her head. "His death is not your fault, Kate."

"Is it not? I should have left the moment I made my decision about working with Jameston, or at the very least insisted the others leave. I so wanted to make my father proud and prove to him he could rest knowing his business was in capable hands."

"Even though it is not what you want?"

She watched a magnificent buck cross the meadow and stop at the stream for a drink. When he raised his regal head at the sound of voices nearby, the impressive animal stared directly at her, as water dripped from his closed mouth. Seconds later, he bounded from view. "Did your grandfather want you to take over his farm?"

"No."

Katharine raised a brow in skepticism.

"He might have harbored the dream early on, but he was happy for me when I made the choice to become a doctor to heal. There was a light of pride in his eyes I had never seen before."

"You are fortunate to have such support."

"Your father loves you, Kate."

"Yes, he does." Katharine's gaze wandered, and she thought the landscape was more golden than when she had arrived. An unmistakable chill hovered in the air as it had not before. "Do you think they will find the men who killed Stewart?"

"I don't know." Brody eased an arm around her and drew her closer to his warmth. "I am uncertain killing anyone was their goal, just frightening us into leaving. Based on their behavior, I would guess we surprised them by showing up when did. Ramsey's Pinkerton friend will be here soon, and the active territorial marshal has been contacted."

"I want to see this through, for Stewart if no other reason." She sat straight and moved off the bench to give herself a little distance. She had come to rely on Brody's strength and comfort, but right now she needed to think about what came next. "I will need to make arrangements for Bessie to go home. The brothers have already left for Utah, so we will require an escort. Are there trustworthy men who would take on the job?"

"There are. A few of the men from Hawk's Peak will—"

"I do not wish to intrude on the Gallaghers' kindness any further. Is there no one else?"

"There is," Brody conceded. "I will have them find you. You're going with her, aren't you?" He pushed off the bench and walked to the edge of the porch.

"As far as the train, yes. I should return around the same time as the Pinkerton agent."

"You can't travel that distance back alone, Kate."

"Am I not as strong as Brenna and Eliza or as brave as Isabelle, Amanda, and Ainslee? Have they, and many others, not proven women are capable of doing whatever they want? This experience has shattered everything I have ever known about what is proper and accepted. I need to know I have it in me, Finn."

She stepped off the porch and walked toward town.

25

"MISS KIELY!" Forest Lloyd ran to catch up with her as she headed into the general store.

"I'm sorry?"

"Sorry, ma'am." The young man heaved in a deep breath. "I'm Forest Lloyd, ma'am, Orin's son."

"Ah, well, then nice to meet you Mr. Lloyd. Is everything all right?"

"Pa left me in charge of the telegraph office on account he went to help his brother birth a calf. He, that'd be my uncle, has a farm south of town. Pa's got a knack for it. Birthing calves, I mean."

Katharine tried not to create an image of

Orin birthing a calf but to no avail.

"A telegram came for you during the funeral. It was marked urgent, but I didn't want to disturb the service." Forest handed it over and appeared to want to wait while she opened it.

"Thank you for delivering this."

"I figure you may want me to send a reply."

Katharine unfolded the paper and read the missive from her father. "I see." Her father received the telegram about Stewart's death, and if any man could convey emotion over a telegram, it was Branson Kiely. There was no mention of either of her letters. She refolded the telegram and tucked it away in a pocket. "If it is all right, I will come with you now and write one out." They backtracked, walking past Brody's clinic toward the telegraph office. "Do you know who owns the plot of land there across from the clinic."

"Ah, which . . . oh, that. The town owns the parcel."

"Why has no one ever built there?"

Forest scratched his chin and stopped for a second. "Well, now, I reckon 'cause no one wanted to, at least not since I've been old enough to know anything. Heard there was a fella once from Denver who made an excellent offer, but the town turned it down."

"Why?" She stepped up onto the boardwalk in front of the telegraph office.

"He wanted to put in a sporting house." Forest waved the idea away. "Can you imagine? The town voted, and no one wanted to sell it to him. I didn't much see the harm in a sporting house, but it ain't for the likes of this town."

"The townspeople vote on just the land

or all matters relating to Briarwood?"

Forest opened the door and stood aside so she could enter first. "We vote on most things, like the times we've needed a new schoolteacher or how to use town funds."

Katharine accepted the paper and pencil Forest handed to her, considered her words carefully, and wrote out a reply to her father.

> *Bessie is bringing Stewart home. Will send word when I put them on the train in Butte. Katharine.*

She slid the paper across the polished, wooden counter. Forest read the note, gave her a long look, and sat down at the machine to send the message. Before he began tapping out words, Forest said. "The town also votes on things like if the railroad should come."

"Is that so?"

"Yes, ma'am. I look young, but I know things. Turned eighteen last month, and I hear lots of stuff working here."

"I am sure you do." Katharine found the young man rather amusing. "The only direct route would be from the west, and the Gallaghers own that land."

"Just saying, Miss Kiely, the town voted once, when Mr. Jameston first approached Ethan Gallagher some time back."

"And the consensus?"

Forest stood and supported his lanky frame against the counter. "Folks are keen on making life easier, but they don't want the railroad in Briarwood."

"No one ever said," Katharine murmured, except Forest heard her.

"Reckon they wouldn't." Forest returned

to his chair and left her with a few parting words before he got to work. "The Gallagher family . . . they own that land all right, but they consider it the town's land, too. They let us decide."

"Then took the responsibility of fighting with Jameston."

Forest shrugged and faced the machine. Katharine heard the clicking from the long and short taps as she left the office. Her gaze wandered first to the distant mountains that could be seen from almost anywhere one stood in town. She found comfort in those stalwart peaks, much like she did in the sea when she looked out the window at home. Only here, the ranges of slopes and crests offered a barrier or protection or perhaps isolation.

Katharine glanced over at the clinic, took a deep breath, and covered the short distance. She stared at the door for several minutes, knowing the heartache waiting inside. How odd, she thought, that within the same walls, Brody cared for both the healing and dead. It was a comfort, she supposed, that Briarwood did not require a full-time undertaker, and yet for Brody's sake, she wished he did not have to be the one to look after Stewart.

She expected a silent interior to greet her. However, the most angelic sound emanated from above stairs, beckoning her to depart from her task and escape the gloom. Katharine stood at the base of the wide staircase, and after a few minutes, grasped the railing and lowered herself to the second step. With her eyes closed, she listened to the melody from "She Is Far from the Land."

"Rachel sings like an angel."

Katharine opened her eyes and looked up at Brody. "She does. I thought she was asleep when I sang it before."

Brody held out a hand, and when she accepted, he grasped her elbow and helped her up. Once standing, and after a brief stall, he let go of her arm. "She might have been. The mind remembers many things without us realizing it." He removed the apron from around his waist and draped it over an arm. "I didn't expect to see you again so soon."

"I came to look in on Bessie. Is she still here?"

"Down the hall in the back room. She won't leave his side. I've prepared Stewart the best I can for transport, and I sent a wire to the undertaker in Bozeman, but he won't make it before . . . Otis has offered to build a special coffin, lined so . . ." Brody couldn't continue. "When do you leave?"

"Tomorrow." It pained Katharine, more than she expected, to say the words. "May

I visit with Rachel? I want her to know that I will return."

"Actually, I need to check her wound dressings. I was going to call upon Flora, but if you don't mind, Rachel and I would appreciate your presence."

In answer, Katharine walked up the stairs, and listened to each soft footfall Brody made as he followed. She wondered how such a towering man moved about without making much noise. When they reached Rachel's room, Brody motioned for her to wait, and he knocked on the door.

"It's Doctor Brody, Rachel. May I come in?"

As always, Rachel's delayed response lasted a few seconds before she called out through the closed door, "Yes."

Brody stood aside to allow Katharine entry first.

"You came." Rachel tried to smile. "I remember the song."

"I heard." Katharine momentarily forgot about her other reason for coming to the clinic and sat in the chair Brody moved next to the bed. "Doctor Brody is right. You have a beautiful voice."

Rachel shyly darted a glance at Brody, whose back faced them as he gathered a few items from a corner cupboard. Katharine realized then he must keep a small stock of supplies in each room. "Rachel." The young woman returned her attention to Katharine. "Doctor Brody needs to check your injuries."

Brody positioned fresh bandages and salve on the small table next to the bed and within reach. "I've asked Katharine to be here, if you agree."

Rachel drew the quilt up to just beneath her chin.

"I only need to check the two wounds on your left arm and the one on your leg, and if they look good, I can remove the stitches. You'll be more comfortable without them. The others weren't deep and will have healed sufficiently. I can leave you some ointment to spread on them yourself."

Rachel eased the quilt back down to her waist and asked Katharine, "Will you talk to me while he is removing the stitches? A story perhaps?"

Katharine scooted forward a little more. "Of course. What would you like to hear?"

"Anything." Rachel flinched when Brody first reached for the sleeve of her nightgown.

"Why don't you roll up the sleeve?" he said. "The first wound is on the inside of the forearm."

She knew Brody was giving Rachel every

opportunity to make the choices in her own life, even the small ones. The pain and guilt from which Katharine suffered since the day before diminished enough when her heartbeat increased and the tightness between her shoulders eased as she watched him minister to his patient.

"You are from San Francisco?"

Rachel nodded.

"My home is also by the sea in Oregon. I spent many carefree days in my youth walking along the beach or the cliffs, usually when my governess wasn't looking."

The smile on Rachel's face was quick but genuine.

"You are a governess, so you will know what I mean. Children can get into great mischief, and my father told me often that my mischief-making caused more than one governess to leave our employ in the early years. I thought I was a rather sweet—"

Brody chuckled without looking away from his task of cutting away each stitch with careful precision.

"Never mind the good doctor." She winked at Rachel, who now gave Katharine her full attention. "Now, I recall one particularly gloomy day, following a wretched week of more gloom and rain. I had been cooped up in the house for too many days and begged my governess— that would have been Miss Pryer at the time—if we could walk on the beach. She forbade it, of course, thinking it might rain again."

Rachel gripped the quilt as Brody removed the last stitch and asked if he could raise her sleeve a little more to reach the other. She nodded without looking his way.

"Well," Katharine continued, "when it was time for afternoon tea, Miss Pryer left me alone for a few minutes, which was not a common occurrence, to fetch some more sewing thread from her room. I was a naughty child, and I sneaked away down the front staircase since I knew the kitchen maid would bring tea up from the back staircase. I left the house through the doors in my father's study and followed the well-traveled path down to the beach." She leaned in closer and whispered conspiratorially, "I filled my skirt with shells before Miss Pryer found me."

Rachel's smile brightened and she even laughed before realizing it and caught herself.

"It is all right to remember the joy." Katharine shared a glance with Brody. "There now, that wasn't so bad, was it?"

Rachel peered at her arm. The puckered

skin was unsightly now but pink and healthy. Brody had left the sleeve for her to pull back into place, and from the grim expression he now wore, Katharine suspected he did not relish asking Rachel's permission to tend to the last of the stitches. Surprising them both, Rachel blew in and out a few times quickly, and then a long inhale and exhale before she folded back the quilt and sheet. It took her longer to raise the hem of her nightgown enough to expose the long gash, neatly sewn together.

Brody said nothing as he got to work. Rachel recoiled a little at first, but she kept her leg still when she asked, "Do you have another story?"

Katharine gazed upon the young woman. "How old are you, Rachel?"

She spoke past a small catch in her throat. "Twenty-three, last week."

Unable to keep her heart from aching, Katharine kept her eyes from misting too much. "How old was the child you looked after?"

"Eight."

"Oh, what an age. Let me see, another story . . . when I was eight, which was when I first met our Doctor Brody. We both lived in South Carolina at the time." She and Brody stared at each other for several seconds as the import of that sank in. Had she really been so young, and he so old. Perhaps it had seemed so back then, and while she remembered the young man with fondness, she associated every memory now with the accomplished physician he'd become.

"During the war?"

"Yes, it was a troubling time, but as children are wont to do, I found ways to play. My mother and I used to like to go for long walks, and my father would accompany us on Sundays after church. My favorite place was a swimming hole on our neighbor's land. No matter how hard my mother tried, she failed to keep me from sneaking away and ruining dresses in the water."

"Did you have a governess then?"

Katharine thought of the mother who had devoted all her time to her father and child. "No, not then. I am not certain one would have tolerated me."

"To be sure, they wouldn't have," Brody said, adding his own comment to the conversation. He cut away the last stitch and cleaned the wound. "All done."

Rachel recovered herself. "I barely felt anything."

"A good doctor has a gentle touch." Katharine would not say what was most in her thoughts: that most men did not use their hands to harm.

Brody gathered the soiled cloths and medical material to dispose and held it while he asked Rachel, "Have you been walking a bit?"

"A little."

"Keep at it. You must give yourself some more time before your leg is strong enough to put your full weight on it. Keep using the cane."

Brody started for the door, but Rachel spoke his name as he was about to pass under the threshold.

Tears flowed freely from Rachel's eyes, except this time, a brightness akin to hope accompanied them. "Thank you for saving my life."

Katharine waited until she heard Brody's footfalls on the stairs. She handed a fresh handkerchief to Rachel, who accepted it reluctantly. "You saved yourself, too, Rachel."

"That's what Doctor Brody said."

"You do not believe him?"

Rachel shrugged and twirled one side of the white linen around her fingers. "I try not to think about it."

"Then do not. You will when you are ready."

"Doctor Brody said that, too."

They shared a quick grin before Katharine brought up the subject that brought her up to Rachel's room in the first place. "I will be leaving tomorrow, but I will return soon."

"Is this about the woman I heard crying downstairs?"

"Yes. She is a dear friend, as was her brother, who was killed yesterday."

"The boy died down the hall. Tilly mentioned it when she brought breakfast this morning. And the nice older woman.

Joanna?"

Katharine nodded. "Yes, Joanna was also hurt, but the doctor fixed her up." No one her age, she thought, should ever have to wear such a solemn expression.

"Why does the world have to be so evil, do you think?"

"Oh, Rachel. The world is not evil. There are those who commit evil acts, but they do not represent all the world." Katharine walked across the room and opened the double doors leading to the balcony overlooking the edge of town and the meadow beyond. "There is more beauty out there than we will ever see with our eyes, touch with our fingertips, or feel with our hearts. When there is so much of anything so powerful and glorious, there must also be an opposite to give balance, to help us become stronger."

She returned to the chair and held her

friend's hand. "You, my dear girl, will be among the strongest of us all. Please, do not lose sight of your strength."

26

BRODY AWAKENED THE next morning well before sunrise and after only a few hours of sleep. He kept vigil over Stewart's body for several hours after Katharine encouraged Bessie to leave his side and get rest. She would need it for the journey ahead.

His body wanted more sleep, but his mind refused to comply, and so Brody checked instruments, medicines, and noted supplies he needed to restock and patients to visit and check on. He had not heard of Mrs. Derkins needing additional care after the birthing. It had not been the first child she lost before it took breath, but Brody wanted to look in to see how she was healing.

Denny Rowland said he and his family were headed to Nebraska, where a cousin was giving them a place on his farm. Brody had no words of comfort to offer the young father who lost a son, except to wish him well. He made a few notes in one of his ledgers to do more research on tick illnesses, and with time, he might be able to prevent another tragedy like what happened to Otto Rowland.

He would examine Joanna's wound, and unless he wanted to risk taking her threats seriously, he would clear her to move about. Brody needed to visit Hawk's Peak and examine Ethan's wound, though he doubted the man kept his arm immobile, unless Brenna was nearby. He could trust that Isabelle was following instructions to remain in bed for a few days but would check on her as well.

Keeping his mind busy was how he would cope with Katharine's departure today. She told him more than once that she would return, and assured Rachel the same, yet Brody wondered if she could really leave Bessie in Butte to make the rest of the journey home. Once in Astoria, would her father convince her to stay?

Unable to brush away the concern, Brody walked to a corner desk, pulled out a scrap of paper and pencil, and wrote out three short sentences. A pale, blue hue shared the morning sky with what remained of the darkness, so he tucked the paper away until the time when Orin would open his office.

In need of fresh air and to stretch his legs, Brody exited the clinic and immediately felt the chill through his shirt. Ignoring the cold, he stepped down from the covered boardwalk and strolled through town. It had been too long since he'd been on one of his pre-sunrise walks, and he missed the ritual of experiencing the town before everyone emerged from their dwellings. Day in and out, the same people carried on the same business. It was the interruptions to daily routine that made life interesting, even though lately the disruptions were more disturbing than usual.

Noticing a faint light on the second level of the general store, he slowed his walk and saw he wasn't the only one out before the sun. Katharine leaned on the upstairs railing of the deck that ran the length of the front of the building. She looked down as though she had been watching him since he left his clinic, and when their gazes met and held, she broke the connection and went back inside.

Brody held his breath for a few heartbeats before continuing his walk. The sound of a door's click as it opened and closed brought him about. Katharine had wrapped herself in a thick, wool shawl, and for the first time since her arrival in Briarwood, her rich, honey-colored hair fell in smooth waves around her shoulders, held in place by a single ribbon tied at her nape.

Without words from either of them, Brody grasped her hand and together they walked in comfortable silence back through town toward the meadow. He liked to think of it as their place and sensed that like him, Katharine needed to be free of walls, roofs, and doors.

When they arrived at the footbridge, he allowed her to cross first, but she did not stop. He followed, saying nothing until they reached the center of the meadow.

Surrounded by openness, Katharine leaned her head back and stared up at the sky. The fading moonlight cast a beam that made her hair shimmer. Fresh snow had fallen in the mountains, and the earth still smelled damp from the rain they must have gotten during the short time Brody slept.

Drawn to her, whether from exhaustion or a desire too strong to hold back any longer, Brody rounded to the front of where she stood so they faced each other. "Kate."

She opened her arms to him and whispered his name. When their lips met, they scorched and cooled in equal fervor. He held her close, his hands finding a warm fit in the folds of her shawl. When he slowly broke away, her eyes held too many questions for him to answer.

"That felt like goodbye, Finn."

"You've said you need to do this alone, and since you aren't going by yourself, I have to think 'alone' means without me. So, yes, for now it is goodbye."

She trailed one of her long, delicate fingers over his jaw. "It might have been farewell twenty years ago when I was a child with no say on what happens next in my life, but that is not the case now."

He kissed her palm and then held it close to his chest. "Bessie shouldn't travel the length of her journey with strangers."

She leaned into him. "I know. I will go back to Astoria and will see that Stewart has a proper burial. My father took the news hard. He counts on me, Finn."

"You're a wonderful daughter." Brody kissed her brow, then put a foot of distance between them. He heard the rumble of a wagon and saw Otis pull his buckboard around to the back of the clinic with a coffin in the rear. "I need to get back."

"I will come with you." Hand in hand, they returned to town and parted at the clinic. Brody remained out front until Katharine closed the door of the general store. With remorse for the task ahead, Brody went to meet Otis behind the clinic.

"Sorry mess what happened to this fella."

Brody merely nodded and lifted one end of the heavy coffin while Otis carried the other. They laid it out on a long table next to Stewart. It was the one room of the building Brody disliked. Natural deaths, accidents, and the occasional criminal were all a part of life's cycle, and Brody did not begrudge his part in it. He preferred to save a life, but when necessary, he liked to see that they were laid out with as much respect and care as possible, even those who deserved little more than a six-foot hole in the ground.

This was not the first senseless death he'd witnessed, but it was the first that so profoundly affected someone he loved.

"How's Miss Kiely doing? The other lady, Bessie, is his sister?"

Brody did not fault Otis's idle conversation. After all, what did one say when standing over a dead body? "Bessie is in a state of shock, understandably, and Miss Kiely is, well, determined to find the person responsible."

Otis removed his wool cap long enough to scratch the top of his head. "Heard Tom say a Pinkerton is coming to Briarwood. Never had one of them here before."

Progress and changing times are inevitable, Katharine would say, but he wondered how well their town would hold up against shifting winds. "It is another matter for which the detective is coming."

"That girl up in the clinic?"

Brody looked askance at Otis. "I hope no one has been spreading tales. The girl has a right to her privacy."

Otis held up both hands. "I didn't mean no disrespect, Doc. We all know how you feel about keeping folks' business private, and we appreciate it. Just been thinking maybe there's more we can do for her."

Duly put in his place, Brody offered an apology. "It's good of you to think of her. If I am cross, well, it is not your fault."

"Begging pardon, Doc, but you've been a might out of sorts since your Miss Kiely came to town. Folks have been thinkin' maybe you don't want her to leave."

Brody used to find the townspeople's penchant for gossip and assumptions amusing. Of course, he'd never been the object of such talk before, and it bothered him now because the tales held a tremendous amount of truth. "Let's get him taken care of." He put an end to the line of conversation about himself and Katharine, and with Otis's help, Stewart, already wrapped in layers of burlap, was laid out in the tin-lined coffin. "This is fine work, Otis. I'd be obliged if you send me the bill."

"That's mighty nice of you, but Miss Kiely, she already paid."

Yes, Brody thought, she would consider it her responsibility. "Well, then. Will you come by when it is time for them to leave? We must send them to Butte with a wagon that Ben can bring back."

"Ben Stuart's going with them?"

They both heard voices at the front of the building. "He is. Thank you again, Otis." Brody left the blacksmith and strode to the front porch. Ben was helping Amanda down from her horse when Brody stepped outside. "Good to see you both. I appreciate this more than I can say, Ben. You, too, Amanda. I didn't expect it, but I'm grateful they'll have another woman with them."

Amanda smiled graciously. "It has been too long since I had a little adventure."

It always felt good to be surrounded by friends, Brody thought, and wished again it were he going with Katharine. "You might tell me how Ethan and Isabelle are getting along before I ride out there later."

Ben laughed and said, "Ethan's been riding, but Brenna's kept him from doing anything to mess up your hard work, Doc. He's not happy about it."

Amanda offered an update on Isabelle. "She is feeling better. The tea you gave her has helped." Amanda looked around at the quiet town. "We arrived early so Ben could speak with Tom. Is there anything I can do to help here?"

"Katharine and Bessie are still at the general store, and I expect my other patient is still asleep."

Amanda pointed to the second story of Loren and Joanna's place. "I see lamps are lit already. I will go and offer assistance." She leaned in for a quick kiss from her husband and made her way down the road.

Brody experienced a quick cut of envy. "You're a fortunate man, Ben Stuart."

Ben grinned. "I never deny it, though most days I wonder how I got so lucky. You all right, Doc?"

"Just a little tired."

"And worried, I'd guess." Ben tethered both horses to the hitching post and stood companionably next to Brody. "We've been out twice more looking for any sign of the other women Rachel mentioned."

"You found nothing?"

"Colton found signs of multiple horses, not carrying a lot of weight each, leaving the mine to the west and leading back onto open land. Where the horse trail left off, a wagon trail started. They're right, Brody. It's not likely her sister or any of the other women are still in the territory."

"Ramsey said as much directly to Rachel, but she won't give up hope of finding her sister." Brody allowed himself a few minutes to enjoy his favorite time of day. "The weather's going to hold at least."

People began emerging from their homes. Brody's section of town, where the clinic took up most of the space, remained quiet, except for a single rider who passed them and stopped in front of the general store. Brody thought of the quaint village in Ireland where his grandfather had farmed and his parents had managed a small shop of their own, selling local produce and notions. It had always been the home of his memories, and of his heart, yet this was where he wanted to be. Despite all the changes coming, he wanted to help the people he thought of as family face the challenges that awaited.

"Have you seen that rider before?"

Brody returned from his past and looked to where Ben pointed. The rider was trying to look through the windows. "Can't say I have. Loren won't open the store for another hour."

Ben did not offer parting words but headed for Loren's shop. Brody wanted to follow but heard a noise behind him. Horses joined the sound of wagon wheels moving over hardpacked earth, and Brody saw a short procession driving down the road on the north side of the meadow. After a few seconds blocked by the church and a grouping of pine trees, they emerged and rounded the corner.

An impressive coach led the procession and was accompanied by a wagon and three riders. They slowed their pace the closer they got to the buildings. Brody stepped back up on the porch, for despite his impressive height, he never did like to give strangers an advantage. The first rider to reach him pulled his horse to a stop.

"We're looking for Miss Katharine Kiely."

"Who is looking for her?"

"I am."

The door to the coach swung open, and just as he'd been when he first saw Katharine, he felt as though twenty years had slipped away. "Mr. Kiely."

"It was always Branson to you, Finnegan."

Other than a dusting of gray at his temples, Branson Kiely still possessed his thick hair, a shade darker than daughter's. He stood a few inches shorter than Brody, with a back ramrod straight and did not appear at all like a man with failing health. Brody grinned and held out his hand to shake, but Branson pulled the larger man into a hug instead.

"It's been far too long, my boy."

"It has, sir. You'll have to explain what you're doing here. Katharine said you haven't been well. A weak heart."

Branson waved away the concern. "My daughter worries far too much and that doctor of mine wants any chance he can take to send me another bill."

"You weren't ill, then?"

The older man hedged. "I am not ill now."

"Glad I am to hear it." However, Brody

remained skeptical. The physician in him wanted to be certain while the man who once shared a bottle of Jameson's with Branson could not bring himself to contradict the man's assessment of his own health. "To be here now, you would have left Astoria before you received Stewart's first telegram."

Branson's demeanor sobered. "I would not let my daughter come out here alone, regardless of what she thought was happening. We've been in Butte the past week, so my manager wired me there whenever a new telegram came through. A bit of a deception, but I had to be sure my daughter was well. You understand, Finnegan."

"I do." Brody shook his head in bewilderment and pointed down the road. "You'll have to come up with a better explanation than that for Katharine."

Branson smiled wide while his daughter rushed toward them, her expression one of astonishment. "Father! Whatever are you doing here?" Katharine waited until they enjoyed a brief embrace before lowering her voice. "How are you? And your heart. However did you survive the journey? And . . . you slept outside, Father." Her voiced held touches of both admonishment and amazement.

"As I explained to Finnegan, you worry far too much. I am well, my dear. We left Butte as soon as I got word about Stewart and made camp last night at a farm with a wonderful family. We weren't far outside Briarwood, but our guides insisted on stopping."

"A family by the name of Dornan, perhaps?" Brody asked.

Branson's eyes brightened. "That was them. We will stop off again on the return trip. Good people."

"They are. I delivered their youngest girl last year." Brody saw they were drawing some attention and invited them inside. He waited until Branson and Katharine had entered the building before looking down the street to check on the rider, but he saw neither him nor Ben. He said to the man still on his horse next to the coach, "You can leave your horses, plus the coach and wagon, around the corner at the livery. Otis will take care of you and your stock, and Tilly's Café opens early. You'll probably smell the food before you see the building."

The man thanked Brody and led the others away. When Brody could no longer see them, he joined father and daughter inside.

27

"I WANT TO see him."

"Father, no."

Branson held his daughter gently by the shoulders. "My dear, we have much to discuss, but that man was a dear friend, and I will pay my respects now."

Katharine did not need to be told to stay behind. The questions she wanted to ask piled one on top of the next and she did not know where to start. For now, she respected her father's privacy and remained in the entry while Brody escorted Branson to the back of the clinic.

She had seen the coach and wagon from the window in her rented room, and when her father alighted from the coach, an overwhelming relief soon succumbed to confusion and perhaps a little disappointment. Too anxious to linger in one spot, Katharine found herself in the surgery room, not at all surprised to find it tidy and every surface clean. There had been little time on previous occasions to admire how much the space reflected the man who spent so much time there.

Bessie would appreciate Branson's arrival, if for no other reason than another link to home. Guilt Katharine had tried to stifle rose once again. She knew intellectually she was not to blame for Stewart's death, yet her heart could not reconcile the part her decisions played.

"How did you learn to move about so quietly?" she asked before she turned to find Brody only a few feet away.

"You heard me."

"It is more that I sensed you." She crossed the room to admire the cabinet of herbs or so it would look like. Really, she needed the distance to keep her mind clear. "Has my father told you anything? I cannot imagine him making the journey. He would have had to leave—"

"Soon after you did."

"I thought he trusted me and believed in me to help him with his business."

Brody invited her to sit on one of the long benches before he joined her. "Trust has nothing to do with his decision to follow you here, Kate. You are all he has left. Can you not imagine the fear he might have felt to send you off alone to a territory that is still feral in most respects?"

"Did he say where he has been all this time?"

"Butte City. He arrived there a few days after you did."

"Yet he did not follow me . . ." Katharine thought about the telegrams. The one where she told Stewart to inform her father about Finn Brody would have been sent around the same time her father stopped in Butte.

"Kate?"

"Stewart disliked my habit of putting too many words in a single telegram." She smiled at the memory. "Since my father has not been in Astoria, then he would not have received my letters."

"You can tell him now."

"Tell me what?"

Branson moved into the room. Katharine always admired the way her father's commanding presence caused all activity to stop. "My letters. You did not receive them. The second one would only just now be arriving in Astoria."

Brody laid a gentle touch on Katharine's

shoulder before saying, "I will give you some time alone."

Branson leaned over as Brody passed, and for the doctor's hearing only, he said, "We need to speak later."

"Your daughter intends—or intended— to leave today with Bessie and Stewart."

The older man's eyes brightened a little, though his smile was faint. "I do not believe, son, that she will go anywhere." Branson patted Brody on the back. "I will find you later."

Katharine watched the quiet exchange with interest, and once Brody left the room, she asked her father to join her on the bench. "I do not even know where to begin, Father."

"Oh, my dear." Branson settled in next to his daughter and leaned against the wall behind him. "You are so much like your mother. I should have spoken of her more often, and for that I am sorry."

"What do you mean?"

"When you came to me about coming here, I already knew."

Katharine narrowed her eyes. "For how long?"

"A few days. My lawyer is quite loyal."

"Then why—"

Branson held up a hand to ward off her question. "Please, allow me to explain."

Katharine smiled when she realized his long pause was because he thought she would interrupt again. "Go ahead."

"You wanted to do this on your own."

She did not deny it.

"I have watched you struggle this past year. You have been with me in every meeting, on every project, and when at home, you were always concerned with my care. I wanted to see my young girl, as you were as a child, a spirit free to explore.

Just like your mother."

Taken aback, Katharine shifted to face him better. "Mother gave all of her time to us. She indulged me, to be sure, but a free spirit?"

"She was that and more, and had she lived, your mother would have sent you away from home long ago, regardless of how much I might have wanted to keep you close."

"What are you saying?"

Branson pushed himself off the bench and peered down at his daughter. "You should finish what you have started here wherever it may take you next."

Katharine stood next to her father and grasped his hands. "Bessie, and Stewart—"

"I have plenty of men with me." He puffed out his chest a little. "I believe even Bessie will approve of an old man like me to serve as escort."

Her eyes awash with subtle tears, Katharine leaned up and lightly kissed her father's cheek. "You are not old. I am sorry I ever thought you incapable, but now I know none of this was about the spur, was it?"

Branson waggled his finger. "Not necessarily. I believe there is opportunity here, and while I will trust your judgment about Mr. Jameston, his participation is unnecessary."

Katharine eased away and released her father's hands. "There will not be a spur line over the Gallagher land. I gave them my word that we would not pursue the matter."

"I see." Branson scratched his jaw and studied her. "Then it is not business that has kept you here."

Overwhelmed now by everything that

had transpired these several days, Katharine sat back down none too gently and thought of the content of her two letters. "There is much to tell you." Mustering all the emotional strength she was able, she rose again. "Tilly serves the best pie I have ever tasted. Why don't we enjoy a slice of her apple-cherry pie while I tell you all that has happened? I am told Tilly serves pie from breakfast to supper."

After all, Katharine thought with no small amount of grief, life must move forward.

Katharine completed her retelling of all the pertinent details since her arrival. Her father's impassive expression gave nothing away, except for the occasional raising of an eyebrow or slowing down his bites. He remarked more than once on Tilly's delicious pie and even gained Tilly's attention when she passed to offer her the compliment directly.

Branson Kiely knew how to charm and win over an audience of twenty or one, and from the café owner's response, Katharine knew he had done it again. "Father. You've said nothing."

He discreetly wiped his mouth with a cloth napkin and then looked directly at her. "I have been trying to think of what I could say. Had I known any of this could happen, I assure you, freedom be damned."

"Father!" she admonished and looked around them. He had spoken quietly enough so no one else heard.

"Forgive me. I have it in my mind to send a dozen men up to deal with Jameston right and proper."

Katharine dismissed the angry threat. "You would not." When he didn't respond, she asked, "Would you?"

"My dear, a man does not get to where I am in business without putting some force behind my threats, but no," he quickly assured her, "I would do nothing, nor have I ever done, to harm another. There are ways, though, and by the time I am done with this Jameston, he will never do business with anyone again."

Perhaps it would not be a bad thing, Katharine mused. No doubt the Gallaghers had similar thoughts, but their influence did not extend beyond the territory, nor did they have her father's business connections. "I promise, Father, that everything I have said of that man is true, so do what you will."

Branson stood and moved behind Katharine to pull out her chair. "Come, let us walk off Tilly's fine baking, and then I would like to see Bessie."

"She has been inconsolable. When I left her earlier, she was packing our trunks." Once outside, Katharine slipped an arm through her father's and guided them down the boardwalk. "I promised her I would go with her to Astoria."

"You leave Bessie to me." He pointed to the general store. "Is that where you have been staying?"

"In the rooms above. Oh!" She stopped and faced him. "There is no hotel in town. There are two vacant rooms above Loren's store, but there is no place for all the men who came with you."

"We will leave today, so there is no need to fret."

"Today? Father, you only just arrived." Katharine stopped herself from implying that a man of his age needed to rest and recuperate after a long journey. His amused smile told her he guessed what she was thinking.

"It is difficult for you to accept that I am capable of many things. Besides, I have a small army of men, including Atman, so I am well looked after."

"Your butler accompanied you? Mr. Atman detests anywhere that is not Astoria."

Branson nodded. "So he has informed me many times. I worked out all the details before leaving Butte—interesting place—and you have work still to do here, or am I mistaken in that the Pinkerton agent will arrive any day. Then there is the young woman, Rachel, who from the way you speak of her, is counting on you."

Every argument Katharine was going to use in favor of leaving vanished. She wanted desperately to seize the opportunity her father was offering, even if remaining meant dealing with unpleasantness. Had she not told Brody that she was strong enough and brave enough to do this on her own? She referred to traveling, and yet so many "what-ifs" fought for her undivided attention.

Her heart ached with the thought of not being there to comfort Bessie, to be with her for Stewart's funeral . . . "I cannot do that to her."

"Well, the choice is yours, Katharine." Branson gave a gentle pat to her cheek and looked at the front of the general store. "This is it."

She had not realized they had continued walking. "I will think about what you've said. Bessie is here."

Bessie opened the double doors wide and murmured, "Loren likes the fresh air."

The spigot of anguish burst, and Bessie bent her head to hide tears cascading down her cheeks. "I am so sorry, Mr. Kiely. I do not mean to cause a scene."

"There, child. You're entitled. Let us walk, shall we?"

Branson escorted Bessie away from the store, having no direction other than walking until the younger woman dried her tears. Katharine watched on, uncertain what to do with herself. She was seeing a side of her father she had always known existed but somehow overlooked. He reminded her now of the time after her mother died, when he buried his own grief long enough to give all his care and consideration to her. At what point, she wondered, did they switch roles?

Her attention shifted from her father and Bessie to the two riders coming from the north. It was unlikely to be anyone from the mine taking that route, which meant Hawk's Peak. She could not tell from here, but by the height of the one on the great black horse, she suspected Ethan Gallagher had decided he was healed well enough.

"Miss Kiely?"

Ben walked toward her, another man striding alongside him. "Mr. Stuart." She had forgotten her lapel watch when she hurried to greet her father earlier but guessed the time to be close to nine o'clock in the morning. She nodded toward the approaching riders. "This is not a coincidence, is it?"

"No, ma'am." Ben introduced his companion. "This is Julian Frank from the Pinkerton Agency."

"Ma'am."

Mr. Frank tipped the edge of his hat. He did not look like Katharine imagined a

Pinkerton agent to look, though having never met one, she had no basis on which to make a comparison. Rough clothes and a somewhat disheveled appearance were more conducive to a miner than a detective.

Ethan and Ramsey brought their horses to a standstill a few feet from where they stood. Ethan, without his sling, swung off his horse. Katharine saw that he still favored his injured arm. Both men offered their greetings first to her, and then Ramsey acknowledged the newest arrival.

"Julian. Good to see you." Ramsey accepted Mr. Frank's handshake. "You made better time than I expected."

"I was in Buffalo, and the main office got me word of your wife. Ben here took me over to your sheriff's office, and they caught me up on what you've learned from the woman, but I'd like to speak with her."

Ethan asked Ben, "You ask Katharine yet?"

Katharine looked at Ben. "You need something from me?"

"As Julian said, he needs to speak with Rachel before he heads up to the mine. Brody just told us you'd better be there, and only Julian can go up with you."

Katharine wanted to ask where they had been when they spoke with Brody, for she had not seen him since he had left her and her father alone to talk. "Mr. Frank. I am happy to oblige, and I know Rachel wants to help in any way you can, but she is still quite fragile."

"Doctor Brody explained, ma'am, at least what he could. I only have a few questions for her and then I'll leave."

His kind voice decided her, and if Brody had already given his permission, then Katharine would also help. She searched up and down both roads to see if Brody was within sight, but she did not glimpse his tall form anywhere.

"Katharine."

She accepted Ethan's help off the boardwalk to the road and instinctively gravitated closer to him as the small group walked to the clinic. Once there, she bid the others to remain outside and turned to the Pinkerton agent. "Mr. Frank."

"After you, ma'am."

28

KATHARINE PAUSED JUST outside the recovery room door and kept her voice at a whisper. "How much do you know, really, that happened to her?"

Julian spoke, equally soft in tone. "I've pieced most of it together. Unfortunately, ma'am, this isn't the first time I've heard of something like this happening. It's a lot to ask of a stranger, but I'm asking you to trust me."

"Ramsey trusts you," was all Katharine said before she knocked on the door. Rachel did not hesitate as long this time to say, "Yes." Katharine opened the door and quickly introduced her companion.

"Rachel, this is Mr. Julian Frank, the Pinkerton agent Ramsey mentioned. May he speak with you? He's here to help find Mary and the other women."

"You'll find my sister?" Rachel did not waver in the intense stare she gave Mr. Frank. Her wide eyes and fine sheen of perspiration across her brow attested to her anxiety.

Katharine remained close while Mr. Frank stood a few feet beyond the foot of the bed. "He's going to do what he can, Rachel."

"I want to go with you," Rachel blurted with abrupt finality.

Mr. Frank's lips creased, and he cleared his throat before responding. "You can't go where I'm going, Miss Watson, but I will make you a promise. I won't give up until I find your sister."

Katharine noticed he did not promise to

find Mary alive. Rachel clasped her hands beneath her chin as though getting ready to pray in thanks. Katharine knew Rachel would continue to hope that Mary will be found alive, and neither she nor Mr. Frank said anything to the contrary. Hope healed better than worry and doubt, and Rachel still had a lot of healing ahead of her.

Mr. Frank took his promise a little further than Katharine expected he would when he said, "No matter how long it takes, Miss Watson, I will find your sister."

With eyes wide and shining, Rachel nodded. "Thank you." She clutched a fist to her chest. "You have questions."

"I will keep this brief, but I wanted to see if you could recall anything else about Mr. Jameston's behavior on the day you met him."

Rachel darted a glance between Katharine and Mr. Frank. "Jameston. Yes,

I remember. I told Ramsey that I met him in Butte."

"How did you meet him?" Mr. Frank asked.

"The older couple who brought us to Montana introduced me."

"Just you?" Katharine asked, then mouthed an apology to Mr. Frank for interrupting.

He smiled in return and indicated Rachel should answer the question.

"Yes, just me. I was coming out of the mercantile, and the others were already in the wagon ready to leave. I can't remember their names."

"That's all right. Take your time."

"Wait. Arthur and Lola Clemmons." Rachel's breath shuddered, but she continued. "They introduced me to Mr. Jameston and said he was an old friend. He then walked me to the wagon and helped me up. He was truly kind."

"Did the Clemmons's stay with you after Butte?"

Rachel crossed her arms under the quilt and shook her head slowly. "No." She tilted her head to one side, then the other. "Yes. I'm sorry."

"Nothing to be sorry for, Miss Watson."

"Yes, they were with us for a short time. Mr. Clemmons drove the wagon and horses, and his wife sat next to him. We were laughing at a story she told us when . . ."

"That's really good, Miss Watson," Mr. Frank said with a great deal of compassion in his voice. "Did anyone else travel with you besides the couple?"

Rachel pulled the top quilt up until it covered everything except her face. "A guide. Arthur and Lola called him Slade." Her eyes flooded with moisture. "Is Mr.

Jameston a part of this? He was so nice."

Mr. Frank surprised Katharine by walking to the other side of the bed until he was only two feet away from Rachel. "You've done nothing wrong, Miss Watson."

Katharine started to come to Rachel's defense when she heard the other woman quietly repeat the words, "What have I done? What have I done?"

"If Mr. Jameston is behind any of this, I promise justice will be served."

Katharine believed him, and in a grand step, Rachel reached for Mr. Frank's hand. "Mary is only nineteen. I used to have a picture of her. You'll find her, I know it." Rachel released his hand.

"What does Mary look like?" he asked.

"Pretty like you, I should think," Katharine said.

"No, Mary is the pretty one." Rachel

smoothed a bruised hand over her own fair locks. "Mama used to say Mary's hair is like fresh cream, and she has our mother's eyes, almost like when the sky doesn't have a cloud anywhere in sight and the sun is so bright it hurts."

"I know the color well." Mr. Frank hesitated when he would have offered a gesture of comfort. Instead he pulled away just enough to give Rachel a little more space, though he had made sure she remained in control of the situation the whole time.

A flush suddenly crept across Rachel's cheeks, and Katharine drew the visit to a close. "Is there anything else you need to ask, Mr. Frank?"

"Please, call me Julian." Looking only at Rachel, he said, "Just one more. How did you get away? Did they leave you alone?"

She shook her head as though in a daze.

"My fingers touched the rock, and I didn't think. Is it wrong for me to hope he's dead?"

"No, it's not wrong. You'll hear from me soon, Miss Watson."

"It's Rachel. It will help if I can think of you as a friend in this because a friend would do whatever is necessary to bring my sister back."

Julian held his hat against his chest and bowed his head briefly. "Then consider me a friend."

Katharine waited for Julian to exit the room first and then excused herself so Rachel could tend to her needs. She held a finger against her lips when Julian looked her way and preceded him down the hallway and stairs. "Why did you ask how she got away? The trauma of recalling—"

"Miss Kiely—"

"Katharine, please."

Julian nodded. "If I had to put together the entire story with what she told Ramsey, and what she said just now, I'd conclude that what her sister heard was the couple talking about what comes next for the women. I would then deduce that the guide, Slade, seized an opportunity, or they gave her to him as payment. Whatever the case, it will be better for her if she gets as much out as possible. Wounds shouldn't have a chance to fester too long."

"You have a cold way of breaking down what might have happened."

"It's the world we live in." Julian's frigid words almost masked the anger Katharine detected on the edges of his voice.

"I don't recall any of the men saying they found anyone who could be this Slade."

"No, they did not."

Katharine reeled at the idea that Slade

could still be out there. "In your experience, do men like him return for their victims?"

"It's possible. They haven't found the man who shot at Joanna or took Rachel from the clinic." Julian walked a few more feet down the hall. "I've seen all kinds of motives, and half of them don't make much sense. If I were a guessing man, I'd say the gun shot was a distraction and taking Rachel was the only goal. With any luck, Slade will have been the guy who threw the knife at Ethan."

"How would that be lucky?"

"I'm told Gabriel got off a shot, which means whoever injured Ethan is dealing with his own wound right now." He motioned for her to walk in front of him as they descended the staircase. Brody had returned to the clinic and waited at the base of the stairs.

"Everyone else is in the kitchen." Brody pointed in the right direction for Julian's benefit. Julian thanked him and left them alone. "How did she do?"

"She did well, Finn. Great considering."

"Then why does it look like you've been crying?" He ran a thumb across her cheek.

Katharine pressed both palms to her face and took a deep breath. "I didn't realize I was. She wanted to go with him to find Mary. He settled the matter efficiently, but I worry about her. It will take some convincing to keep her here."

"Your father found me."

The abrupt shift had Katharine straightening her back. "My father found you? You have spoken with him again?" she asked with uncertainty.

"I did, only briefly. He told me you won't be leaving today with them."

Katharine paced the narrow space and

tapped a finger to her palm with each point she made. "My father *told* me I should stay, but he did not wait to find out if I was going to *listen*. Bessie and Stewart deserve better from me than to stay behind while my friend deals with her loss alone. My father does not listen, Finn. He is shrewd, yes, and wise, and of course he will give Bessie every care possible on the journey home and see that she is looked after."

Brody halted her pacing and swung her around to face him. His raised brow and gentle smile caused her cheeks to flush. "You do not have to tell me I am behaving like a petulant child who isn't getting her way."

"You are behaving like a woman worried for her friend and a daughter concerned about her father. None of us have the answers to what comes next. Will the decision you make today to stay here affect what happens tomorrow? You know it will, but how do you know staying isn't the right choice? You argue that you're strong enough to go, but are you brave enough to stay and finish what you've started?" He answered his own question in the next second and shook her gently. "I *know* you are."

"You read me so well, but that isn't all of what weighs on me."

He brushed loose hair from her face and kissed her disgruntled frown. "It's guilt."

Katharine nodded.

"No one can tell you how to feel, Kate, but remember I was there, and you have no reason to feel guilty."

She looked over her shoulder toward the kitchen, and her eyes widened. "There is something I can still do to see that Stewart gets justice." Katharine walked down the hall and into the room where Ethan, Ben, and Amanda were speaking with Julian. She directed her first question to Ethan. "Eliza went home before I could ask, but did she mention anything about right before the shooting started? I recall her starting to say something, an idea she had, maybe."

"As it happens, that's the other reason we're here. Eliza said something to Ramsey." Ethan rolled his injured shoulder and rubbed the base of his neck to ease some of the stiffness. "Say nothing, Doc. It's a twinge is all. The arm is healing fine." To Katharine, he said, "None of us have had a good look at that plot map since our parents passed, which is why we hadn't considered the possibility that Jameston could tunnel under our land."

Ben said, "If he is, then he's likely found a vein that spreads onto your parcel."

"Which would explain why we caught his men by surprise out there," Brody added.

"We'll make another search of the place, but a warrant to walk the tunnels would be better." Ethan asked Ramsey, "Is that something you can get?" who

Ramsey pointed to Julian. "Maybe, with his help."

Julian nodded. "I'll do what I can, but there's a chance they might blow the tunnel rather than risk getting found out. If they hear about the warrant too soon, there's a good chance of that happening, which means evidence of encroaching on your land, and whatever metals or minerals they have found, will be gone."

"I don't give a—" Ethan glanced at the women.

Katharine exchanged a smile with Amanda and brushed away his concern. "Please don't hold back on our account."

Ethan gave her a half-smile before finishing his response to Julian. "I don't care about whatever they've found. My family has no intention of mining on our land. Not now, not ever. The mine has given good jobs to a lot of good men, and they don't deserve to get caught up in what's about to happen, but unless honest people take over, I'd just as soon blast the whole operation."

"Let's hope it doesn't come to that." Julian secured his hat in place. "I'll be heading out now for the mine. If the mine takes me on, then it will be a few days, maybe a week, before you hear from me."

"You're going to work at the mine?" Katharine asked. "Is it not risky?"

"These investigations work better when the one under scrutiny doesn't know it."

Julian said his goodbyes and departed, leaving Katharine with more questions than she had before. "Ramsey, if you manage to get a warrant, and Mr. Jameston is arrested, what happens to Rachel's sister and the other women with her?"

Ramsey didn't hold back the truth. "It's possible Jameston will talk in exchange for leniency but unlikely because that would open him up to additional charges. He'll spend the rest of his life in the territorial prison, if he's lucky, for his part in the kidnapping, and whatever else, of those women."

Katharine's lips trembled when she spoke to Ethan. "Knowing what little I have learned of you since my arrival, I assume you will say, 'To hell with the land and the mine and find the women.'"

Despite the seriousness of the question, Ethan flashed her a quick smile. "That's about the size of it, Katharine. To hell with everything else. Just find the missing women." His smile dimmed. "Heaven help them with what they must be going through."

Stewart's cheerful face flitted through her years of memories. She wanted justice for him specifically, but he would tell her that justice for the women would tip the balance far enough in favor of truth and right, so nothing else mattered.

29

"YOU'VE DONE WELL, my dear."

Katharine embraced her father's affection and held him close, and for a moment the action transported her to her childhood. "I'm not done, Father."

He held her face in his hands. "None of us are." Branson let go when Otis brought the wagon carrying Stewart's coffin around from the back of the clinic. "It's time, then."

"You can't stay one night?"

"The undertaker in Butte is expecting us." Branson kissed her brow and moved away to speak with Brody. "I always liked you, son, and in all the towns in all the world, you end up here."

Brody chuckled. "Your daughter said something similar shortly after she arrived."

"She can take care of herself."

"She can, and a lot of others, too."

Branson held up a finger at the same time both his brows raised. "But she'll do better with someone to help her along the way. You must know that it isn't easy for me to leave her here."

"You aren't leaving her here, sir, you're letting Katharine find her own way." Brody removed the note he was going to wire that morning before Branson's arrival and passed it to the older man.

"What's this?" Branson unfolded the paper and read the hastily scrawled words. Katharine's father embraced the younger man in a quick, but fierce hug. "When I return, I expect to find her truly happy."

Brody looked over Branson's shoulder and smiled at Katharine, who clutched Bessie to her as the two women said their farewells. "It will be her choice, sir."

"You know her well, Finnegan. You know her well." Branson patted his shoulder and returned to the coach and his daughter. "This is a pleasant town, Katharine. Could be there's opportunity here, yes?"

Katharine considered the large parcel from where she stood. It backed up to a grassy area and not far behind the stream offered a quiet place beneath a giant tree whose green leaves were fading into a beautiful shade of yellow. She would ask Brody if he knew the species of tree. "There is." She sidled closer. "And not just for me, Father."

"I met Ethan Gallagher, and I see now what you meant." Branson looked around him. "These are good people, Katharine, but as I have been reminded, the choice has to be yours to leave or to stay."

"Thank you for saying that." Katharine kissed her father's cheek. "You already know my choice. I cannot explain it all now, but I will write often and send telegrams in between letters."

With a touch of joy mixed with sadness around his eyes, her father said, "This isn't goodbye, my dear. I expect to hear about your plans for this little town."

"I won't be taking over, Father. More like enhancing."

Branson Kiely shrugged with a smirk and helped Bessie into the coach before turning back to his daughter. "I have always found partnership to be far more lucrative than going at it alone." He climbed into the coach behind Bessie, sat in the opposite seat, and pulled the door closed.

Katharine had to admit that whatever her father's reasons for following her, the journey appeared to have done well by him. It had been a long time since she had seen him so robust. "Be well, Father." She reached in and took Bessie's hand. "You be well, too. I will miss you."

Bessie's eyes were dry now. "My brother wouldn't be blaming you any more than I do over his death. You and your father gave Stewart the best years of his life, and I ought to know."

"Will you stay on at the house in Astoria?"

"For a time. We have a cousin in St. Augustine, and I do like warm weather." Bessie gave her a bright and genuine smile. "Perhaps we'll both find our own adventures."

Incredibly touched, Katharine took back

her hand and steepled her fingers in front of her mouth as the coach turned in the wide road, followed by the two wagons and riders, and headed out of town.

Brody came up behind her and encircled her waist. "For a minute there, I thought you might change your mind."

"For a minute there, I considered it." She continued to watch the procession of wagons and riders until they rounded the corner and faded into the landscape. "I do not know why I ever considered him frail."

"Trust that he knows what he's doing, and I think he wants to take care of this task personally. Your father's sense of responsibility to his people runs deep, and it wouldn't be right to deny him that. Besides, I remember him as a man who thrived on challenge."

"You're right." She covered the hand over her hip with her own. "What did you give my father before he hugged you?" It was a pleasurable site for her to see his cheeks flush.

"It was a telegram I planned to send this morning."

She waited for him to elaborate, which he did not without prodding. "Is it a secret?"

"No, but it isn't time yet, either."

"I will not beg, but you have piqued my curiosity."

He held out his hands. "Begging would not become you." Brody smiled. "Besides, it will do no good."

A slow smile formed on her lips. "I would be disappointed if it did. Will you join me? I want to speak with Rachel about what comes next. It's not feasible for her to remain at the clinic once she is well enough to get around normally. I thought to speak with Loren about continuing to rent Bessie's room for Rachel but have not yet had the opportunity."

"She has to want to stay, Kate."

"You are good at letting others make their own choices. You do not prod or try to convince them of one way or the other, so let us give it a go, shall we?"

Brody led her to the porch. "I learned long ago that a person is more likely to heal from an injury or find the power to fight off a terrible illness, if they decide for themselves that they want to get better. All I can do is tend to wounds and heal the body using all my skills and knowledge."

Katharine entered the building first and walked backward a few steps so she could keep eye contact. "Does it never frustrate you?"

"All the time." He grinned. "Especially when I'm treating a member of the Gallagher clan."

She laughed while removing her hat and jacket. She still had her hair loose around her shoulders like in the morning. A thin ribbon the same color as her skirt kept some of it back and away from her face.

Together they walked up the stairs and down the hall to Rachel's room. The door was open for the first time since Rachel had returned.

"What are you doing?" Katharine rushed into the room. Rachel had changed into a calico dress Katharine had purchased a few days ago from Loren's store. It hung loose at the waist, and she needed several more substantial meals at the café.

Rachel bent over a little to look under the bed. "Has Julian left already?"

Brody walked to Rachel's side and acted without thinking. He gently helped her stand upright, then immediately dropped his hands. "You shouldn't be bending over like that, at least not for a while."

She sucked in a breath and let it out slowly as fresh tears formed in her eyes. "I didn't think." Rachel sat on the bed and beat a fist into the mattress. "I need to be there when he finds Mary."

Katharine knelt on the floor in front of Rachel. "Julian is going to the mine. Now, I cannot say what will happen, but infiltrating the mine as he plans to do could be dangerous."

"My sister and the other women won't be there. Everyone thinks so." Rachel put her hand directly over her heart. "I know it in here. They were gone long before that man—Colton, I heard someone say— found me running in the woods. How will going to the mine help?"

"I do not know how an investigation like this works, Rachel, but Julian made you a promise. He will find your sister, and I believe him." Katharine started to rise and was helped the rest of the way by Brody. She untangled her skirt and sat next to Rachel. "Were you ever separated from your parents as a child, even if you only lost sight of them for a few moments?"

Rachel nodded.

"Did you try to find them, or did you wait until they found you?"

"It was my sister who ran away from us, but I understand. She waited for one of us to find her, just like our parents taught."

"That's right." Katharine wrapped an arm around her friend. "If you stay here, then Julian will always know where you are when he locates your sister."

Rachel looked around the room. "I can't stay here indefinitely, and I can't be idle. I'm already going mad from it."

"There will be a safe and quiet place for you above Loren's store when you are ready to leave the clinic. I will be in the room next door, so you will not be alone."

Surprise etched on her face, Rachel asked, "You aren't leaving?"

It was the first moment since she decided to stay that Katharine truly felt it was the right thing to do. "No, I am not leaving." Eager now to speak with Ethan Gallagher again, and with Brody about her idea, she asked, "You won't attempt to leave? You will wait?"

Rachel shook her head. "I'll wait, for now."

That was all she could hope for, Katharine thought. "I'll be back soon."

Once outside, Brody easily caught up with her. He had stayed long enough to make sure Rachel had what she needed. The young woman's decision to stay now made, even though she had a little nudge from Katharine, she wanted only to sleep.

Brody considered it a good sign.

"Kate." He slowed his long strides now that he had reached her side. "Where are you going?"

"I am looking for Ethan."

"He headed back to the ranch already."

Katharine halted in the middle of the road. "You are certain?"

"I watched him leave with Ben and Amanda. What is this about?"

"I have an idea. Several ideas, in fact, and one of them will require a partnership. Will you ride with me out to Hawk's Peak?"

Brody did not try to resist the allure of her contagious eagerness. "This is important to you."

"Yes."

"I'll go with you tomorrow morning if you wish. We can leave early, but it's going to be dark before we make it back."

"My father—"

"They didn't have much choice in leaving right away since Bessie was insistent on getting Stewart back to Astoria for burial. Besides, your father won't be on horseback, and they are stopping at the Dornan's farm for the night." Brody lifted her chin, and she immediately stilled. "It has occurred to me we haven't had a proper meal together yet."

"No, we have not."

With his hand around Katharine's waist, they strode to the café, where Tilly was already doing a bustling business.

———⚬⚬———

Brody met Katharine, as promised, in front of the general store the following morning. He arrived a few minutes early to find her in conversation with Flora Carver, though he recognized the signs of someone impatient to extricate themselves.

"Good morning, ladies."

Flora bobbed her head. "Good morning to you, Doctor."

"Miss Carver—"

"Flora, please."

Katharine smiled and said, "Then please call me Katharine. Flora was just telling me about her upcoming visit to Salt Lake City."

"Oh? I didn't know you were planning a trip, Flora, and this late in the year."

"My cousin is to be married, and I promised her I would be there." Flora quickly added, "I know my time away will leave you without help, but it's only two weeks. I don't want to close the school for any longer than necessary."

"It is time I try to hire a nurse. You have your students to attend." Brody held out his hand for Katharine, but she remained, watching Flora walk away.

"You mentioned difficulties before finding a nurse." Katharine accepted his hand and stepped down to the road.

"The right person will come along." Brody heard the double meaning in his words, though neither remarked on it.

"I could help until you find a suitable nurse."

Brody did his best to keep his grin subdued. "I'd like that, and folks would appreciate it, but are you sure?"

"I will be a poor substitute for Flora or Joanna, who both have some training—"

"Training is only part of it." They stepped around a mess left behind by a horse and continued to the livery. "There's a lot of change coming. You said it was inevitable, but this is good change."

She smiled up at him in a way that made him feel ten feet tall and like the most important man in the world. "Yes, wonderful change is afoot. I only hope the Gallaghers agree."

"You still haven't told me your idea for them."

Katharine straightened her lips and became serious. "You can beg."

The gleam in her eyes gave her away. He gently nudged her as they approached the livery. "Careful or I might."

They found Otis removing shoes from a pretty, gray horse while the large space filled with warmth from the heating forge. "Doc. Miss Kiely. What can I do for you this fine morning?"

Brody said, "I'll get my own horse out, but we could use the loan of that mare Katharine borrowed before, if she's available."

Otis wiped sweat from his brow, despite the chill in the morning air. "I'll get her saddled."

Half an hour later, the tops of the buildings at Hawk's Peak came into focus. They'd made good time, and not once did Katharine ask to slow down or complain about discomfort. They slowed as they approached the arch to the ranch entrance. "You're a finer horsewoman than you originally let on."

"I suppose one never forgets how, and I loved riding when I was younger. I don't know now why I ever stopped." She paced her mare at a slow trot, and Brody held his larger gelding back a little to keep the same clip. When they reached the main house, Brody dismounted first and then helped her down.

Ethan stepped out onto the porch with

Brenna. Wearing his hat and a duster that skimmed just below his thighs, Ethan appeared ready for work. "Katharine. Brody. What brings you out here? Everything all right?"

"You can see from their faces that all is well, am I correct?"

Brody shrugged and Katharine smiled.

Brenna brushed past her husband and held out a welcoming embrace to them. "I am glad you came, no matter the reason. Come inside. Ethan has been telling us what has happened in town yesterday and of your father's visit and departure. You've seen a lot of activity during your brief time in Briarwood. Reminds me of my first weeks here." Brenna winked at her husband.

Katharine's skin held a nice rosy hue, and Brody knew excitement for the future and not exhaustion from the past several days brought on the heightened color. "She has something urgent to speak with Ethan about."

"Urgent?" Ethan's brows furrowed, then smoothed out. "From the way you look, Katharine, I'd say your urgency in this instance is a good thing."

She lifted the hem of her skirt enough to ascend the stairs. "I hope you think so after what I have come to ask of you."

Brenna looped her arm with Katharine's and ushered them inside. "Breakfast is finished, but Amanda made some delectable scones if you have time for tea."

"We have time," Brody said and stopped when Ethan held out a hand in front of him.

"You know what this is about?"

"As it happens, she hasn't told me yet, and why ruin the surprise?" Brody chuckled and joined the women inside.

A bewildered Ethan sat across from them twenty minutes later. He rubbed the back of his neck and considered her proposal. "A partnership with you and your father? In what?"

"A train depot and holding yard for cattle and horses."

Ethan leaned against the back of the sofa he sat on with Brenna. "We already told you no spur line will cross that land."

"Yes, and I gave my word that we let that idea go, nor will we pursue it again. I do not wish to run tracks on your land."

Ethan leaned forward a little. "All right, then what are you proposing exactly? You can't have a train depot without a train."

"You can, if the depot is built, say, halfway between Butte and Briarwood. Kiely Limited can build the spur no farther than the depot. The holding yard will be for the cattle from the area brought to market and easier transport for your growing horse trade. The difference of a day or two will save considerable time and resources for the smaller ranches and farmers and make life a little easier for the people in Briarwood with transportation and supplies."

Brenna said to her husband, "This is rather fortuitous."

Brody noticed the subtle look of concern in her eyes and wondered what it was about. "It would be good for the town, Ethan."

Curious, Katharine asked, "What do you mean by fortuitous?"

Ethan sighed. "She means this is something Gabriel, Eliza, and I have spoken of before. Just last year in fact. We made inquiries but weren't able to get anyone interested in building a spur line to the middle of nowhere."

With her shoulders and back straight as a stick, Katharine pointed to herself. "I am interested. Or, more importantly, Kiely Limited is interested."

Ethan slowly nodded. "It will take significant backing to accomplish what you're recommending, and we won't risk any part of the ranch as collateral."

"That is why I am hoping for a partnership. This is what my father does, Ethan, and it will be an excellent investment for everyone involved, without destroying the land or infringing upon the town."

"A section of the land the spur would have to cross is privately owned, some of it federal."

Katharine's lips curved again. "My father is quite good at what he does. I made the mistake of underestimating him recently, and his fleeting visit yesterday reminded me that too often opportunities vanish before we realize the lost possibilities. I do not want to let this one pass either of us." She stood, and the others did the same. "My purpose today is to plant a seed of an idea and to see where it takes us. Your family knows the land and what it will take to bring about progress without destroying what you love most about this place. I hope you will think on my proposal, and if you are agreeable, I will wire my father with the details."

Ethan waited long enough for Katharine to start biting her lower lip and dart glances back and forth between them all. Ethan first met Brody's gaze, who silently offered his blessing, then turned to Katharine. "It sounds like you're planning to stay in the territory for a while."

Katharine eagerly shook his hand. "Yes."

Brody lifted her one last time for the day from the back of the mare. The sun was making its descent behind the snow-topped peaks surrounding the valley when they returned. They had made good time on the return ride. A chilly wind ruffled Katharine's loose hair to the point where it skimmed over his face. He held her longer than necessary before releasing her.

"I'm proud of you, Kate."

"I am a little proud of me, too, if it's not too bold to say."

"Not at all." He led the horses into the livery where Otis was banking the fire in his forge. "If I can make use of your stables for a few minutes, I'll brush them down."

Otis took both sets of reins. "No need. You take that nice Miss Kiely to Tilly's. Heard she made berry cobbler for dessert."

"Thank you, Otis."

Brody appreciated the convenience of having the livery around the corner from his clinic, though he would need to think about making some changes. He returned to Katharine's side and repeated Otis's suggestion that they have dinner at the café.

"I would like that."

Once they were seated at a table by the window in Tilly's, and their orders for the meat loaf dinner and berry cobbler placed, Katharine asked, "If I want to speak with the entire town, who can bring that about?"

The meat loaf and fluffy biscuits arrived, prompting a delay in Brody's response. "The reverend usually organizes any town meetings, seeing as how they're held at the church, but tell a few folks and the rest will soon know." He inhaled the savory aroma and took his first bite. "Is this about another one of your ideas?"

She also took a bite and savored. "She is an amazing chef. Yes, it is, and it has everything to do with the empty land across from the clinic."

"Brody!" The sheriff held up his hand and half trotted toward them. "I've been looking for you both."

Brody asked, "Everything all right, Tom?"

Tom pointed over his shoulder at the jail. "The Wright cousins are fighting over that bull again." He handed Katharine a piece of paper. "Another telegram's come through, and I thought you should see it, for Rachel's sake."

Katharine held the telegram so both she and Brody could read it.

Jameston dead -(STOP)-
Found in mine shaft -(STOP)-
Can confirm tunneling under
land -(STOP)- Investigation has
changed -(STOP)- Tell Rachel I
keep my promises.

"I can guess what he means by the last sentence but figured you ought to be the one to tell her, Miss Kiely."

She nodded and returned the telegram. "Is there hope of finding the women without Jameston's cooperation?"

"I've heard tales of Pinkertons spending months on a single case. If those women are out there to be found, they'd be the ones to do it." Tom tipped his hat to Katharine, nodded to Brody, and offered a goodbye before heading into the livery.

"I worry Rachel will not take this well, Finn."

"You worry she'll try to leave?"

Katharine splayed her hand on Brody's chest. "I should speak with her now."

He caressed a finger over her cheek and smiled. "I'll have Tilly send over some food."

A few minutes later, Katharine entered Rachel's bedroom, surprised to find the door slightly ajar and Rachel sitting in a chair by the window with a book in her lap. Her attention, however, was not on reading.

"Rachel?"

The book dropped to the floor when she bolted upright. Rachel pressed a hand to her chest and bent to pick it up.

"No, let me." Katharine rushed over and performed the task herself. "Brody said you weren't to bend yet." She dropped the book on the chair. "I am sorry to have startled you."

Rachel shook her head and took a calming breath. "It wasn't your fault. My mind has been drifting all day."

"You may want to sit back down." Katharine pulled up another chair. "Mr. Frank sent a telegram to the sheriff."

Rachel's trembling hands rested on her lap. "What has he found?"

"Mr. Jameston was found dead in one of the mine shafts. We have no more information than that right now." Before Rachel could panic, Katharine was quick to add, "Julian's telegram also said to tell you that he keeps his promises."

"He said that?"

"Yes." Katharine saw that the news did not remove all of Rachel's newfound worry and with good reason.

"What do you think will happen now?"

"I think—no, I believe with all my heart that Julian will find your sister."

Rachel rocked back and forth, with her pained stare fixated on Katharine. "You truly believe she is alive?"

Katharine prayed she was not offering false hope, but her father had told her to trust her instincts. "I do because I know hope makes us stronger than fear. Please, give Julian the time he needs."

Rachel slowly nodded. "I still do not know what to do with myself. All I do is think about Mary and what might be happening to her."

"Those thoughts will not help either of you." Katharine stood. "As to what to do with yourself, I want to share an idea with you."

A few days later, Brody and Katharine sat in the front pew of the church while the reverend held up his hands to signal it was time for everyone to be quiet. The church was full, from front to back, with many of the men standing along the side walls.

"Quiet, folks." Once everyone settled, the reverend said, "Now, most of you have heard about Miss Kiely and some of what has transpired since her arrival. We're not here to talk about any of that, so no questions on the whole affair, but she would like to speak with all of us on another matter."

The reverend moved aside, and Katharine took his place in front of the group. She picked out faces she recognized, including those of Ethan and Gabriel and others she'd met at Hawk's Peak. Drawing comfort from those familiar to her, Katharine did not bother to ease into her reason for bringing everyone together. "I would like to buy the empty parcel across from the clinic."

Silence fell over the townspeople, with only Brody smiling. He already knew her intentions. Ethan and Gabriel both offered her encouragement with their steady glances and nods.

"Whatever for?" Loren asked. Joanna, thankfully, sat next to him and no longer looked pale.

"An inn. Briarwood needs one, and I want to build one."

"An inn?" someone from the back called out. "Not much use for one here."

"There could be. I have not been here long, and most of you have heard stories about my reasons for coming. Some true, and others maybe not, but I can assure you that I have the best interest of the town, and all of you, at heart." She cast her eyes over Brody. "Progress is inevitable, but it is not something to fear."

Murmurs arose, filling the interior with noise. Brody stood in response, and everyone immediately quieted. "Let her finish."

Katharine steeled her defenses and thought of what her father would say, then smiled when she realized she only needed to speak from the heart. "The inn would provide a few jobs and would be large enough to hold town events. It won't be fancy or out of place. I hope to provide lodging for weary travelers and visitors to Briarwood. Giving them a place to stay might encourage them to spend a few days in town, which would bring business to the local merchants."

"What about feeding them?" another person asked from the group. "We already got Tilly's."

Murmurs of agreement moved through the church. "Yes, you do, and better food I have not tasted in all my travels. Tilly and I will speak later, but I promise that the inn will not take away business from anyone. I want to work with you and for Briarwood."

Ethan made his way to the front of the church, and everyone hushed. "If Miss Kiely will allow me to interrupt." She stepped back. "You all know how much I dislike even the mention of progress."

Rumbles of agreement followed.

"Not this time," he said to a shocked audience. "She doesn't know this yet, and I'm humbled to be saying it, but Miss Kiely has convinced me and my family of her resolve and commitment to this town, and if you give her a chance, I think she'll convince all of you, as well. You see, we plan to build a train depot far enough from town to keep our way of life, but close enough to make that life a little easier."

Ethan gave her control of the conversation again, but he did not leave the front of the church, and Brody did not take his seat again. Two stalwart protectors, one a new friend, and the other a new love, and between them Katharine had found a home. She faced the audience again as they lowered their voices and became silent once more. "In my short time here, I have learned that one's commitments and promises matters a great deal to you. I have chosen to remain here, and I promise you that whatever I do will benefit the people of Briarwood."

Otis pushed off against the wall he'd been leaning against. "I say let her buy the land."

"I second that," Tilly called out from her spot in one of the middle pews.

Katharine listened as they talked amongst themselves. They did not all know her yet, but they would. They would come to know the woman from Astoria by the sea, who arrived with a naïve plan and eager spirit, a woman who found peace and contentment on the wide, open range. She hoped to be their neighbor and have them recognize her as the woman who stumbled into their town and offered her a place to renew her spirit.

The reverend called for a vote, and they raised their hands one by one, until the decision was unanimous. Katharine believed it was Ethan's words and Brody's defense of her that helped the town decide, but it did not matter how it came to be. She planned to uphold her promises to the Gallaghers, the town, and Rachel. Her eyes drifted over once again to Brody. She had one more promise to make.

The reverend shook her hand and assured her they would see to the details of the sale soon. Katharine thanked him, and with Brody's guidance, departed through the rear door while everyone else exited through the front.

The enclosed space had been more difficult to handle than she realized until the cool air caressed her skin. "Thank you for believing in me, Finn."

Their hands brushed once, twice, and the third time he held on. "I always will. It will take some time to complete these plans of yours. I, for one, hope it's going to take a really long time."

She gave him an indulgent smile. "There is my father to consider. Seeing him briefly after our temporary separation was nice, but it will be longer now. Winter is coming and soon Christmas. He hosts a grand party every year for his employees and their families, and this is the first year I will miss it. His business has flourished every year, which means more people. He'll stay busy, and he has friends and business acquaintances, but it isn't the same as family. I am his only family, Finn."

"You promised to write your father and wire him regularly."

Katharine nodded. "I did, which will help us both. Oh, and Rachel will have a place at the inn when it's ready, though I pray Julian finds her sister before then. I spoke with her and think she will agree, if only to fill the days while she waits for news. In the meantime, we can keep her busy. She has an education and could do well here. There will be much to accomplish over the next several months."

"You've a good heart, Kate, with a kind spirit. You were there for Rachel in a way no one else could be. Something in you spoke to her, and I believe she recognized the goodness in you. You helped with the Rowland children and Joanna when she was shot. You didn't hesitate to step in to help when needed, and you worked tirelessly by my side, bringing comfort and compassion to the patients."

"You are the healer, Finn, not I."

He pressed a hand to her heart. "Healing is more than instruments and medicines. Give Rachel time to decide what is best for her. In the meantime, and with winter coming, your inn will take many months to plan and build. There's plenty of time for us to visit your father."

Katharine whirled around to face him. "You would go with me?"

Brody shook his head in amazement a second before he pulled her back into arms. He kissed her as he had imagined during so many restless nights and quiet moments. They melded together as two people should, fitting a mold created by God and nature. He smiled against her lips before releasing them. "You haven't figured it out yet, have you? I can't do the asking this time, at least not yet."

"My choice?"

He kissed her hand. "Always."

"You and my father both said I should finish what I started, but it is not merely about being strong enough to make a change but also to move forward and be brave enough to take a risk." Katharine bundled his larger hands between hers. "I choose you to ask me."

Brody laughed with abandon and lifted Katharine off the ground and into his arms. "Miss Katharine Kiely. Will you do me the greatest honor of sharing your life and your heart with me?"

"Always, Finnegan Brody. Always." Katharine thought of Brenna's advice that day overlooking the Valley of Dreams. *Every moment of joy we can capture is in our right, be it one minute or one day.* She intended to followed Brenna's advice every day for the rest of her life with Brody.

30

"I DON'T THINK this looks right."

Amanda pointed a flour-covered finger at the edges. "You need to press those in like the one we made last week."

"Yes, I remember now." Katharine pressed her fingers into the crust dough around the edge of the pie dish.

"Your mind is elsewhere."

Katharine rotated the dish a little at a time, pressing even indents as she went. "I suppose it is. Thank you for all the cooking and baking lessons and for moving the lesson to the clinic today. Brody has a young patient upstairs who had an operation yesterday, and I want to be close in case she needs anything." Katharine knew it was unrealistic to think another child would never suffer and die the way young Otto Rowland had, but she wanted to be around for the successes.

Amanda formed the dough into rounds and filled two bread tins. "I hope nothing serious."

"Appendix. Brody said she's recovering well." Katharine finished the crust and checked the oven's heat before sliding the pie inside and closing the iron door. "To think, I didn't even know how to properly work a stove or boil water before I came here."

"You wouldn't guess it now." Amanda wiped flour from her hands, covered the two bread loaves, and placed them near the hearth to rise. "The reverend will probably ask you to contribute to the spread at the spring social."

"If spring ever gets here," Katharine mumbled as she wiped evidence of their afternoon of baking from the table into a metal pail.

Amanda laughed while she dunked a cloth into warm, soapy water and followed behind Katharine's cleaning. "It has been a hard winter already, but it's only January. I'm afraid you'll have to wait a while longer for spring. Ben and I passed your land this morning on the way in. The new stable looks nice."

"The builder has tremendous talent. They'll start on the house and inn, once the weather allows." Katharine checked the oven heat again. Her last attempt at baking alone resulted in a cake hard enough to chip a tooth. "How much longer, exactly, for the snow to stop?"

Amanda laughed. "A few months, maybe four if winter decides to linger. What are winters like in Astoria?"

"Cold, but not like here."

"You never traveled with your father in the winter?" Amanda asked.

"No, we were always home, and now I know why." Katharine surveyed the kitchen and found nothing out of place. "It is beautiful outside, though."

"It is. How is Rachel handling it? That is where your mind has wandered today, hasn't it? I heard about the letter from Mr. Frank."

Katharine had been thinking of little else since Julian's last letter to Rachel had arrived. He promised to keep her informed, and he did so with regular missives or telegrams, often lacking detail, but those letters gave Rachel hope. "It has been longer this time, and Rachel worries that means something terrible has happened."

Katharine lifted the kettle off the stove and poured hot water over herbs into two teacups. "It doesn't have to mean something bad. Perhaps he is in a place without a telegraph office or a way to send mail."

"That is what Brody told her when she was here yesterday." Katharine listened for any sound that her husband-to-be might be moving around in his office, but all was silent in the clinic. "She is doing well, all things considered. I'm grateful with how kind everyone in town has been toward her."

"As far as we're all concerned, she is one of us now. Loren and Joanna treat her like a daughter." Amanda relaxed in a chair at the table. "The tea is ready. What are you looking for out there?"

"Not what . . . who."

"Who then?"

When she stood at the correct angle near Brody's clinic kitchen window, she could view passersby and new arrivals in town. "Eliza and Gabriel are here." Katharine strode into the entry hall and opened the front door before either one on the other side knocked. "This is a pleasant surprise."

Eliza gestured a hand over her shoulder. "Isabelle pleaded with me to take him away for a little while."

"Pleaded is not how I would put it," Gabriel said in defense of himself.

"Fine, she begged me." Eliza brushed snow off her coat and removed her hat before entering first.

Brody said from behind Katharine, "How is Isabelle?"

"Better than ever and resting as instructed." Gabriel also swept snow off his coat before following his sister inside. He hung his hat on a hook near the door. "She asked me to pick up some more of that tea you brought last time. Seems this kid is taking longer to get here than August did."

Brody chuckled. "You'll meet your son or daughter in a couple more months. In the meantime, I'll send you back with a good supply of tea."

Eliza stuffed her gloves into her pockets and offered a hello to Amanda when she joined them. To Brody she added, "We brought the other thing you wanted. It's a day early, but Ramsey had unexpected business in town."

"Vague," Katharine murmured and peered up at Brody. "Is this another secret?"

"Until now." He grinned and lifted her long, woolen, winter coat off one of the hooks. He helped her into and then donned his wool-lined overcoat. "Would you like to join us Amanda?"

"Oh, yes. I don't want to miss it."

Brody helped Amanda into her coat and the small group shuffled outside, with the door closed firmly behind them to keep out the cold. Gabriel disappeared around the corner of the building and returned a few seconds later with a graceful, gray mare.

"She's beautiful!" Katharine approached the horse and held out her bare hand near its nose. "Is she the secret?"

"She's yours." Brody rested his hands on Katharine's shoulders. "An early wedding present."

"Finn." Katharine said his name with reverence and smoothed a flat hand over the mare's face and mane. "What's her name?"

"I'm told Andrew already christened her, but you may choose whatever you like."

Katharine smiled as she recalled Isabelle telling her that ever since Andrew named Gabriel's horse—Zeus—he became the designated name selector at the ranch. "What does he call her?"

"Duchess," Eliza said with a grin. "Apparently it came from a history lesson on British royalty."

Katharine spoke softly to the mare. "Are you Duchess?" The mare bobbed her head, producing a laugh from everyone. "She's well trained."

"Ramsey and I have been working with her for the last year."

Katharine almost asked Eliza if she really wanted to part from the horse, then thought better. Hawk's Peak produced the finest horses in the territory, as evidenced by the pretty mare before her. "Is she a thoroughbred?"

"Descended from, but she's what we call an American Saddlebred," Eliza answered. "Brody wanted you to have the best."

"She is that." Katharine leaned up and kissed his cheek. "Thank you, Finn. I will cherish her." She then said to Eliza, "And thank you and Ramsey. I could not have asked for a more precious gift, and now that they have finished the new barn and corrals, she'll have a nice new home with Brody's horse." She didn't have to wonder at the timing, for the builders had finished the barn only two weeks ago before a new storm swept through. It would be months still before their house was built, but well worth the wait. "We can get her over to the new—"

"Katharine! Brody!"

Rachel rushed toward them, waving a piece of paper in the air. Gabriel saved her from a tumble when she slid to a stop on the wet snow. "Sorry, Gabriel."

Katharine brimmed with pride and love at how far her friend had come in the past few months. Rachel did not cringe or shy away from Gabriel's brief touch. "What's happened, Rachel?"

"This." She handed Katharine the telegram. "Forest delivered it to the store a short while ago. I only just returned from Tilly's and—" She took a deep breath. "Read it."

Located Mary -(STOP)- We're coming home.

"This is wonderful news, Rachel."

"Yes, it is, but weeks with no word and now this. He says nothing of how he found her or where." Tears trailed down Rachel's cheeks. "We've been apart four months."

Brody opened the clinic door. "Let's take this inside."

Gabriel gathered the mare's reins in one hand. "I'll take her over to your barn. Is your gelding already there?"

Brody nodded and thanked Gabriel for them both. Katharine was absorbed with assisting Rachel inside. They gathered in the kitchen, the only room comfortable enough for all of them. Amanda moved over to the stove and placed the kettle back on the heat while Katharine helped Rachel into a chair. Brody selected calming herbs from the cupboard and passed them to Amanda.

Eliza had removed her coat and joined them. She sat in the chair next to Katharine and was the first to speak. "Delivering the mare isn't the only reason we came to town today. I planned to do this with Ramsey present, but I don't know how long his business with Tom will take."

"What's going on, Eliza?" Brody asked. "What was Ramsey's unexpected business?"

"Julian has been keeping Ramsey informed. I'm sure Julian's left details out of his communications with you as a kindness, Rachel." Eliza rested her arms on the table and leaned closer to Rachel. "You already know that the new owners up at the mine have cooperated with the investigation into Jameston's death. Ramsey is with Tom today because the person who did it finally came forward. It was a wife of one of the miners."

Rachel did not retreat into herself, but it was close. "I don't think I want to hear this."

"You should, though. Turns out Jameston facilitated these miner-bride introductions before. This woman was one of those brides a year ago, and she ended up with a good man, but her story is otherwise similar to yours. She kept quiet on threat of her life. She was content with her new husband and so she stayed."

"Then why now? How long has she been there?"

"Seven months. Somehow she heard about you and decided if you were strong enough to fight back . . . well, as she put it, she broke. She got lucky with her husband but never recovered from what happened to her before then." Eliza left the rest unsaid and clutched Rachel's hands.

"You have already spoken to her?"

Eliza nodded. "Gabriel, Ramsey, and I were there this morning. News will spread through town quickly enough, but Tom wanted to keep things quiet until he had a chance to wire the territorial judge. We all agreed you deserved to know, which is why we were coming to see you next."

Katharine's eyes misted, and she recalled Brody telling her that a dear friend of Eliza's, many years ago, had died after a comparable experience. "What will happen to this woman?"

Eliza released Rachel and leaned back. "Only she and Jameston were in that mine shaft, and no one is going to fight for him. She admitted lying to Jameston to get him there, but after we produce all the evidence against him, Ramsey is confident a judge will rule it self-defense."

Rachel wiped her tears. "When did she turn herself in?"

"Yesterday."

Rachel pushed back her chair and stood, ignoring the tea Amanda had poured for her. "I want to speak with her."

Eliza also rose. "I'll take you over. Tom

is letting her use his rooms above the jail until they sort this out."

"What of her husband?" Brody asked.

"She got quiet when Tom asked the same question. It seems she never told her husband what happened. Tom said Doug Carlson is a good man, so we'll see."

"Lena Carlson killed Jameston?"

"You know her?" Eliza asked.

Brody nodded. "I treated Doug's leg injury this summer."

"Well, Jameston isn't around to ruin any other lives again, and that's all Lena said she wanted." Eliza scoot in her chair. "I'll remind Gabriel to stop back by for Isabelle's tea."

"Eliza, wait." Rachel followed her into the hallway. "Mary is coming home, and nothing else should matter, but I need to know where she's been. You said Julian has kept Ramsey informed with more details. Have those details included anything else you can tell me?"

"Last I heard, Julian was searching mining camps in Colorado. He received word from a sheriff down there who heard something from someone else. It took Julian a while to find the source of the information. That's all I know." Eliza donned her coat and hat.

Rachel re-buttoned the jacket she had not removed earlier. "I've heard stories about your family."

Eliza paused and slid her hands over her leather gloves. "Go on."

Katharine stopped short of where Eliza and Rachel stood, not wishing to interrupt, yet compelled to stay when she heard the generous kindness in Eliza's voice.

"You—all of you— have seen a lot of bad things, haven't you?"

"We have." Eliza handed the gloves to Rachel, who was too surprised not to accept them. "But no matter how many horrible things we've seen or been through, those somehow fade away. It's the good memories that remain with us."

Rachel slid the warm gloves onto her hands. "You make it sound easy."

"There's nothing easy about life, as you well know. My mother once told me that the good days are God's way of reminding us we're not alone, and the tough days are his way of showing us that alone or not, we're strong enough for whatever we have to face."

Rachel's trembling voice held an underlying conviction when she said, "Mary's going to be all right."

Eliza nodded. "So are you."

"I owe my life to Brody and Katharine, and I'm indebted to your family and

Julian, and—"

"Let me stop you there." Katharine caught Eliza's brief glance in her direction before Eliza continued, "You decided to survive—your choice—and that's worth everything."

Katharine exchanged one last look with Eliza and slowly walked backward as the other women left the clinic. She hit a warm barrier and strong arms wrapped around her before Brody leaned down to whisper against her ear. "Rachel and Mary will both be all right because they're surrounded by people who will make sure of it."

"How much did you hear?"

"This will answer your question." Brody kissed the edge of her cheek. "The best part about you proposing marriage is knowing we'll never be alone, and always be strong together."

Katharine tugged his arms closer. "I didn't propose."

"We'll disagree on whose memory is better."

Katharine repositioned herself and leaned her head back to look directly up at him. "You're a frustrating man, Ardgal Finnegan Brody."

"I got through the last twenty years with no one knowing my first name. How?" Brody squeezed a laugh out of her when she didn't answer. "Quiet now, or you'll give Amanda the wrong idea."

"Amanda is a married woman and understands." The woman in question chuckled and brushed past them. "If I'm not mistaken, your wedding isn't for another two months."

Katharine thought of the promise she gave her father. "We could go to Astoria rather than wait for my father to come here."

Amanda scoffed at the idea as she donned her outerwear. "Your friends in this town will not forgive you." With her hand on the door handle, she smiled and added, "But you can always have two weddings. Don't forget the pie. The loaves will be ready to go into the oven in an hour." Amanda waved a goodbye and left them to the consider her suggestion about more than one wedding.

"We couldn't, could we?" Katharine asked.

"You won't get an argument from me. I wanted to marry you the second you asked. Now, about the name, Kate. No one knows it."

"No one in Briarwood."

He titled his head back as though looking at the heavens. "My grandfather told you."

"I may have written him before Thanksgiving. His letter arrived after Christmas." She trailed her finger up his chest. "He does not mince words, and he has many stories. I swear I could hear him laughing through the letter, were it possible for such a thing to happen."

He kissed her soundly. "Now you know all my secrets."

"All of them?" Katharine smiled as those powerful arms tightened their hold.

"Unless you want me to tell you about the girl I kissed on my grandfather's farm."

Katharine lightly pinched his arm and then smoothed it out. "I've reconsidered this matter of the proposal. I did ask you, and it will be a wonderful story to tell our children."

Brody deliberated for a few seconds. "On second thought, I asked you."

"You're certain?"

He lifted her face a little more and skimmed his lips over hers. "I will be when I repeat the telling of it to our firstborn."

Thank you for reading
The Healer of Briarwood

Visit mkmcclintock.com/extras for more on the Gallagher family, Hawk's Peak, and Briarwood.

If you enjoyed this story, please consider sharing your thoughts with fellow readers by leaving an online review.

Don't miss out on future books!
www.mkmcclintock.com/subscribe

AUTHOR'S NOTE

The name Katharine Kiely is in fact, a real person's name, though everything about the character is fictional. Katharine is a name belonging to the mother of the high bidder in a charity auction for RAINN, which won her a place in one of my books by having a character named after her. She selected her mother for that honor instead. I am grateful to her for her support of the auction and am delighted to use her mother's beautiful name for a character. The heroine's name changed a few times in the early drafts, and it wasn't until she was bestowed with "Katharine" that she truly came to life.

While the surname Kiely was rare in the United States during the 1840s-1880s, census records indicate that there was no Kiely in either South Carolina or Oregon.

Taking creative license, as writers are wont to do, I ignored that little statistic and gave the Kiely family a home in both states.

—⁂—

Julian Frank, the Pinkerton agent introduced toward the end of *The Healer of Briarwood*, owes his fictional name to two real-life Pinkertons, Gustave Frank and Henry Julian.

For more information about Frank and Julian, check out the article, "10 Legendary Exploits of The Pinkerton Detective Agency," by Debra Kelly.

I started researching the Pinkertons for another series that I am working on with a fellow author, set at a later time and in Colorado, and while I did not originally plan to introduce one into the Gallagher series, the characters had other ideas.

The North-Western Police Agency, later known as the Pinkerton Agency or Pinkerton Detective Agency, and now known as Pinkerton's National Detective Agency, has a long and fascinating history. While not all exploits were strictly "by the book," they offered protection, defense, and crime-solving skills to help numerous people over their many decades of service. The Pinkerton Agency was the closest thing to a national police force before the FBI was created in 1908.

A timeline of the Pinkerton Agency history can also be found on their website: https://pinkerton.com/our-story/history.

THE MONTANA GALLAGHERS

*Three siblings. One legacy.
An unforgettable western romantic adventure
series.*

Set in 1880s Briarwood, Montana Territory, The Montana Gallagher series is about a frontier family's legacy, healing old wounds, and fighting for the land they love. Joined by spouses, extended family, friends, and townspeople, the Gallaghers strive to fulfill the legacy their parents began and protect the next generation's birthright.

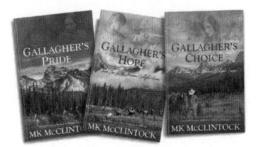

THE WOMEN OF CROOKED CREEK

WHITCOMB SPRINGS SERIES

Meet a delightful group of settlers whose stories and adventures celebrate the rich life of the American West.

Set in post-Civil War Montana Territory, in the mountain valley town of Whitcomb Springs, is a community of strong men and women who have worked to overcome individual struggles faced during and after the war. Escape to Whitcomb Springs with tales of adventure, danger, romance, and hope in this special collection of short stories and novelettes. Each story is written to stand alone.

Available in e-book and paperback.

ABOUT THE AUTHOR

Award-winning author MK McClintock writes historical romantic fiction about chivalrous men and strong women who appreciate chivalry. Her stories of adventure, romance, and mystery sweep across the American West to the Victorian British Isles, with places and times between and beyond. When she's not writing or running her businesses, she experiments with new recipes, plays in the garden, explores mountain trails, and takes a lot of pictures. With her heart deeply rooted in the past, she enjoys a quiet life in the northern Rocky Mountains.

MK invites you to join her on her writing journey at www.mkmcclintock.com, where you can read the blog, explore reader extras, and sign up to receive new release updates.

Made in the USA
Las Vegas, NV
24 January 2021